P9-BHZ-820

"I love the sounds you make," he said against her throat.

"The way you taste, the feel of you . . ." He pushed the coverlet aside and bent to fully savor her.

It was on the tip of Kristina's tongue to say that she, too, loved. And what she loved. But she stopped herself.

She was well aware that she had seduced James into an intimacy he had tried to resist. He was a proud man, and a private one, who was still healing from a harrowing experience.

Later, she told herself, there would be time.

She was wrong. But in that pleasure-lit night, wrapped in firelight and silk, made whole by exquisite passion, she never would have believed how swiftly time could run out. . . .

Dear Reader,

The year is coming to a close, so here at Silhouette Intimate Moments we decided to go out with a bang. Once again, we've got a banner lineup of books for you.

Take this month's American Hero, Micah Parish, in *Cherokee Thunder*. You met him in the first book of author Rachel Lee's Conard County series, *Exile's End,* and now he's back with a story of his own. Without meaning to, he finds himself protecting woman-on-the-run Faith Williams and her unborn child, and suddenly this man who shunned emotion is head over heels in love. He's an American Hero you won't want to miss.

Reader favorite Ann Williams puts her own spin on an innovative plot in *Shades of Wyoming*. I don't want to give anything away, so all I'll say is beware of believing that things are what they seem. In *Castle of Dreams,* author Maura Seger takes a predicament right out of the headlines—the difficulties a returning hostage faces in readjusting to the world—and makes it the catalyst for a compelling romance. Award-winner Dee Holmes checks in with another of her deeply moving tales in *Without Price,* while March Madness find Rebecca Daniels writes a suspenseful tale of a couple thrown together and definitely in danger in *Fog City*. Finally, welcome new author Alicia Scott—a college student—whose *Walking After Midnight* takes gritty reality and turns it into irresistible romance.

And 1993 won't bring any letup in the excitement. Look for more of your favorite authors, as well as a Tenth Anniversary lineup in May that you definitely won't want to miss. As always, I hope you enjoy each and every one of our Silhouette Intimate Moments novels.

Yours,

Leslie Wainger
Senior Editor and Editorial Coordinator

CASTLE OF DREAMS

Maura Seger

Silhouette® INTIMATE MOMENTS®

Published by Silhouette Books New York

America's Publisher of Contemporary Romance

If you purchased this book without a cover you should be aware
that this book is stolen property. It was reported as "unsold and
destroyed" to the publisher, and neither the author nor the
publisher has received any payment for this "stripped book."

SILHOUETTE BOOKS
300 East 42nd St., New York, N.Y. 10017

CASTLE OF DREAMS

Copyright © 1992 by Seger Inc.

All rights reserved. Except for use in any review,
the reproduction or utilization of this work in
whole or in part in any form by any electronic,
mechanical or other means, now known or
hereafter invented, including xerography,
photocopying and recording, or in any information
storage or retrieval system, is forbidden without
the permission of the publisher, Silhouette Books,
300 E. 42nd St., New York, N.Y. 10017

ISBN: 0-373-07464-6

First Silhouette Books printing December 1992

All the characters in this book have no existence
outside the imagination of the author and have
no relation whatsoever to anyone bearing the same
name or names. They are not even distantly
inspired by any individual known or unknown
to the author, and all incidents are pure invention.

®: Trademark used under license and
registered in the United States Patent and
Trademark Office and in other countries.

Printed in the U.S.A.

Books by Maura Seger

MAURA SEGER

and her husband, Michael, met while they were both working for the same company. Married after a whirlwind courtship that might have been taken directly from a romance novel, Maura credits her husband's patient support and good humor for helping her fulfill the lifelong dream of being a writer.

Currently writing contemporaries for Silhouette and historicals for Harlequin and mainstream, she finds that writing each book is an adventure filled with fascinating people who never fail to surprise her.

Prologue

The room fell silent as the man entered. The voices and shufflings of more than a hundred people waiting there died away abruptly. In the sudden hush, the only sounds were the whirring of the cameras as they were switched on and the quick movement of the reporters pressing toward the small dais set up in front.

The man was in his late thirties, tall, broad shouldered, with black hair touched with gray. His features were rugged, the jaw square, the cheekbones chiseled, the nose patrician. His eyes were light blue and guarded. They revealed nothing of his emotions or his thoughts.

He wore an elegant suit that was slightly too big for him and he looked unusually pale, but aside from that he might have been any political or business leader preparing to address a group of eager reporters.

Although all eyes were on him, the man gave no sign that he was perturbed by the intense scrutiny, or even particularly aware of it. He stepped onto the dais and stood slightly to one side as another man approached the podium.

The second man cleared his throat as he looked out at the reporters. Speaking in English with a slight accent, he said, "I have the pleasure to welcome Mr. James Wyndham to Damascus. He arrived here from Beirut by car without incident. As I am sure you will understand, he is tired. However, he does have a statement."

James Wyndham stepped in front of the podium. Flashbulbs exploded as the television cameras whirred. Reporters and photographers elbowed each other out of the way for a better view. He stood for a moment, surveying the crowded room until it quieted down again.

"Thank you, Mr. Foreign Minister. I am very glad to be here. I wish to express my gratitude to the Secretary General of the United Nations and to the British government for arranging my release. It has been a very long four years. I am looking forward to seeing my home again and being reunited with my family. That's really all I have to say."

The reporters ignored that. They were on their feet, shouting all at once.

"Mr. Wyndham, do you intend to regain control of Wyndham Industries after all this time?"

"How do you feel about the rumors that your kidnappers were willing to ransom you but your family refused to pay?"

"Is it true you were traveling in Lebanon on a secret mission for the British government?"

"Were you working for the Americans?"

"Was Wyndham Industries selling arms?"

"Is it true the terrorists tortured you for trying to escape?"

"Do you have any messages for your brother, Richard?"

Slowly, James looked at the reporter who had asked the last question. The corners of his hard mouth lifted in a smile that even the most naive would have called chilling.

"No," he said. "None."

With that, the press conference ended although the reporters continued to shout questions. James, the Foreign Minister and various other dignitaries made their way out of the room.

The television screen set up in one corner of a plush London office flickered as the scene cut from Damascus to the BBC commentator who announced that with the release of James Wyndham, one of the more complex and mysterious hostage stories had entered a new phase. The kidnapping of the British industrialist had never been satisfactorily explained; he appeared to have been targeted for different reasons than other hostages.

His return raised questions about control of the vast Wyndham business interests, which had been the subject of much wrangling among family members during his absence. The commentator closed by predicting that the story would bear continued watching.

As regular programming resumed, Richard Wyndham switched off the set. He slumped back on the leather couch at the far end of his office, staring at the blank screen, and cursed under his breath. In his early thirties, Richard was a slightly shorter and younger version of his brother.

Although the resemblance between the two was striking, his features were softer and less aggressively masculine. People tended to find him pleasant and easygoing. No one had ever found James to be either.

Four years in a Beirut hellhole apparently hadn't changed that. James was as tough as ever and he was coming back. Indeed, he would be on British soil again in a handful of hours. And then . . .

The phone on the desk rang. It was Richard's private line. He got up to answer it himself.

"Dickey . . ." the woman's voice was soft and breathless. She sounded frightened. "Did you see?"

"Of course, I did," Richard said impatiently. What did she imagine, that he hadn't bothered to watch? His manner softened as he thought that she had every right to be concerned. They both did.

"There's nothing we can do now," he said quietly. "He'll be here soon."

"There must be some way . . . something . . ."

"No," Richard said. He wasn't surprised by his own acceptance. Unlike James, he had always been willing to admit when there was no way to win a fight. "We simply have to hope that he will understand."

"Understand?" the woman repeated. Her voice rose slightly. "Understand that you took everything that was his, everything that mattered to him? And that I went along with it? That while he was rotting in some hideous jail, you and I . . . we . . ." She broke off, choking back a sob.

"Tessa," Richard said urgently, "this won't do any good. I agree that James is liable to be extremely angry, but there is nothing we can do. We chose our path and now we are damn well going to have to pay for it."

"That's easy for you to say. You're his brother. He was always fanatical on the subject of family. No matter how enraged he is, he'll be more inclined to forgive you. But I..."

"He won't forgive me," Richard said quietly. His hand tightened on the phone until his knuckles shone white. A pulse beat in his temple. He could almost feel the ground slipping away under him, leaving nothing but an abyss.

James was coming home. His brother. The man he had loved and admired all his life. The man he had betrayed.

"He'll destroy me," he said and then, more softly, added, "just as I deserve."

Tessa was still speaking as he hung up the phone. Slowly, he sat down behind the stark marble-and-glass desk—the desk from which he had struggled for four years to run the far-flung Wyndham empire.

Along the way there had been successes and failures, but overall the experience had not been what he expected at the beginning. No matter how much time passed or how hard he worked, he had never felt like anything more than a usurper.

And now it was almost over. James was coming home.

Richard settled himself to wait.

Chapter 1

Dawn was still an hour away when the dappled gray stallion came to a halt on the ridge overlooking Innishffarin. The horse had run hard over several miles but was still breathing easily. He tossed his head, snorting steam, and whinnied his pleasure.

James Wyndham patted the stallion's back and smiled. Storm had recognized him at once when the two were reunited the previous night. So excited had the big-hearted horse become that he almost kicked the back out of his stall. Only the gentling hand of the sole man he had ever recognized as master calmed him. It had been too late then for a ride but James had promised himself that he would take the horse out at the earliest possible opportunity. Scant hours later, he was keeping that promise to them both.

He had not slept since the plane ride from Damascus, but the lack of rest didn't bother him. On the contrary, he felt energized to an extraordinary degree. But perhaps, he thought wryly, there was nothing extraordinary about it. Perhaps freedom always had that effect.

Freedom. He savored the word in his mind as he touched his heels lightly to the stallion's sides and urged him forward. It was a cliché, but there was truly no more beautiful word. Nor was there any sight more beautiful than the one that greeted his eyes as horse and rider topped the ridge and started down onto the jagged split of land below.

Where land and sea met stood Innishffarin. The vast turreted castle stretched over several acres from the curtain wall that surrounded it on three sides—the fourth being the rocky cliff and the wild sea—to the crenellated keep soaring against the sky. Begun in the eleventh century, the castle had put his family's stamp on the land and proclaimed it their own. Although the Wyndhams had lost ownership of Innishffarin for several generations, they had never lost their identification with it. When an ancestor of James's had reclaimed it in the previous century, a vow had been made that it would never pass out of Wyndham hands again. It stood as a mighty reminder to the courage and endurance of their line.

Wyndham Manor, several miles distant, was a far more gracious and comfortable residence. James had been born there and it was to the manor that he had returned the previous night. Returned alone because he had made it clear he did not want any company.

His brother, the executives of his company, Tessa... He frowned as he thought of them. The scene at the airport had been pandemonium, everyone scrambling over each other trying to convince him how thrilled and grateful they were to have him home.

Everyone, that is, except Richard, who had stood off to one side, grave and watchful.

The brothers had exchanged only a bare minimum of words and none of substance. Richard, Tessa, all of them would have to wait. He wanted—no, needed— this time alone. Barely had he stepped onto Wynd- ham land than he began to feel more himself.

But the manor alone was not enough. It was to the castle on the edge of the sea that he was drawn while the sky still twinkled with stars and the pale vestige of the moon drifted overhead.

Innishffarin. He was not ashamed that the sight of it made his heart beat more quickly. As the broad walls rose above him, he at last allowed himself to believe that he was truly home.

Which was all well and good but for the fact that something—he could not say exactly what—seemed to have changed. Of late, the castle had become a pop- ular tourist spot and museum, home to the famous Wyndham Cross that had been discovered the previ- ous century hidden in a nearby sea cave. For as long as James could remember, visitors had been allowed in three days a week. They came in considerable num- bers, particularly once the soft, fragrant spring set- tled over the Highlands.

It was far too early in the day to find any such visi- tors about, yet there were several vehicles parked off to one side of the castle. As he listened, he could hear the clang of metal from the inner courtyard. A curl of smoke rose above the bailey wall, carrying with it the scent of burning wood.

Scowling, James crossed the wooden ramp over the moat. The portcullis was in an upright position. He passed through unhindered, the stallion's hooves thudding softly on the hard-packed earth. At first glance, everything looked as he remembered it. Directly in front of him was what had been the family apartments, which included a private chapel. Towers rose at each corner, bracketing what had been the great hall, kitchens and barracks. The barracks were now a tea shop serving visitors but apart from that...

The barracks door opened and a man stepped out. He stood, scratching himself lazily as he yawned. He wore a leather jerkin and what appeared to be homespun woolen pants that came no farther than his knees. His calves and feet were bare. His hair fell below his ears and appeared to have been cut with the aid of a bowl. He looked to be about twenty, no older, and well built.

As James watched silently, the young man went over to a trough near the barracks, bent down and ducked his head into it. He came up a moment later, sputtering, and shook himself, sending showers of water in all directions. That done, he took a knife from his belt and proceeded, without benefit of either soap or a mirror, to shave himself. Granted, he didn't try to make much of a job of it, seemingly content to leave a stubble, but James winced all the same.

Storm felt the movement, however slight, and started. At the same time, the young man caught sight of horse and rider. He stiffened, the knife slipped and he let out a yelp as he cut himself.

"Bloody hell," he said, "who are you?"

"I was about to ask you the same," James said. He moved the gray stallion forward until they stood directly in front of the young man. Looking down at him, James frowned. "What are you doing here?"

"Working," the man said as though it should be obvious. He pressed his fingers to the cut to stop its bleeding and added irately, "The castle isn't open, not even to visitors on fancy horses. You can get out the way you came in."

The young man turned toward the great hall, apparently presuming his instructions would be obeyed. When he heard no sound to confirm that, he turned again and looked back at James.

"I said the castle isn't open."

"And I asked who you are and what you're doing here. I suggest you find a civil answer to both those questions and do so quickly."

The young man stopped where he was and stared at James. He saw a tall, powerfully built man atop a mighty horse, a man who looked perfectly civilized in black breeches, a white shirt and an old tweed jacket, and yet who somehow radiated danger. Slowly, not taking his eyes from James, he asked, "Who are you?"

"James Wyndham, which also happens to make me Laird of Innishffarin. It's my land you're standing on and I want to know why."

Under other circumstances, the young man's response might have been comical. His mouth dropped open as his eyes turned saucer-wide. "W-wyndham? You were in Lebanon..."

"I'm back," James said laconically. "Now for the last time, what are you playing at?"

"I'm not playing at anything. I work here."

"In that getup?"

"Hey, this was the height of fashion in the thirteenth century." When James didn't respond, a possibility occurred to the younger man. Slowly, he asked, "Didn't anyone tell you?"

"Tell me what? About thirteenth-century fashion?"

"About what's going on here?"

"That," James said between his teeth, "is what I've been trying to find out, Mr.—?"

"Standish. Francis Standish, but everyone calls me Frank. Well, not here. Here I'm Francis or Standish, Frank not being a given name back then." The discovery that he was talking to the castle's owner had caused a marked improvement in the man's attitude. He was going out of his way to be friendly but succeeded only in baffling James.

"Back when?" He was trying very hard to follow Francis's...Standish's...Frank's train of thought but he didn't seem to be getting very far.

"In the thirteenth century," Standish said patiently. "That's where we are here."

"We are?" Perhaps Mr. Standish was nuts. It wasn't entirely impossible, indeed the more he had to say, the more likely it seemed. Or perhaps the problem was his own. The psychologists who had met with him briefly at the Royal Air Force base outside of London had warned him that all sorts of aftereffects had to be expected from his captivity. But they hadn't mentioned full-blown hallucinations.

"That's the experiment," Standish said. "We're recreating life in the thirteenth century in an effort to understand it better. This is the perfect place for it. Almost all the construction on the castle took place before 1300 and very little has changed since then. Oh, sure, we had to move out a lot of furniture and cut off the electricity and plumbing, but aside from that, it wasn't hard at all. It doesn't take all that much effort to imagine that this really is say, 1292."

"You're clear on the fact that it actually isn't?"

Standish laughed. "We're not bonkers, if that's what you mean, although I can see how we might seem that way. You have to really believe in this kind of thing to stick with it."

"How long have you been here?"

"Two months. Most of the time we've spent getting rid of anything that didn't fit the time period, but now we've begun to live as they did then. It's fascinating."

"I'm sure it is," James said dryly. He thought back for a moment over the four years he had spent largely without running water, lights, or any of the other comforts of the modern world. He had wanted nothing so much as to get back to that world, but apparently there were others who felt differently.

"You aren't on your own?"

"'Course not. I'm just one of the students. If you come along, I'll introduce you to the professor."

Too curious to turn back, James agreed. He hitched the gray stallion to a convenient post outside what had been—and appeared to once again be—the forge and followed Standish into the great hall.

The last time he had been inside the castle, the hall had been a cavernous but oddly comfortable living room with well appointed couches, overstuffed chairs, tables stacked high with reading material, Persian carpets and the like. Now it was starkly different. Every trace of the modern world had been banished. In place of the carpets was the now bared flagstone floor covered with rushes. The only furniture were three trestle tables grouped in a U with benches on either side. Various iron pots hung around the immense fireplace.

A woman was stirring something in one of the pots using a long wooden spoon. She was so intent on her task that she did not hear them enter, giving James a chance to study her before she knew she was being observed.

She was tall for a woman—about five-nine or five-ten and slender, with flaxen hair pulled back in a long ponytail that reached halfway down her back. Seen in profile, her features were attractive if not classically beautiful. Her nose turned up slightly and her chin was more assertive than fashion dictated. She was simply dressed in a homespun chemise under an ankle-length tunic. A leather belt held the tunic clinched around her slim waist.

When she moved, James was suddenly aware of the fullness of her unbound breasts beneath the clothing. He frowned at his body's sudden and unmistakable response. While he was still dealing with that, she turned and for the first time he saw her fully.

Her eyes were hazel, he thought bemusedly, filled with the green and gold of a summer day. Her lips were full and soft. They curved in a tentative smile as she looked at him.

"You're James Wyndham," she said. It wasn't a question, she knew for certain who he was. Moreover, the knowledge seemed to give her pleasure for there was a palpable note of joy in her voice. She let the spoon drop and took a quick step forward. "Welcome home."

She was a stranger, he had never met her before in his life. Moreover, Innishffarin wasn't his home. He had lived most of his life at Wyndham Manor. Yet none of that seemed to matter. The moment the flaxen-haired woman spoke the words, James felt their truth. He was home—here in this great looming pile of hard stone by the sea—and in some strange and sudden way he could not explain, her presence only underscored the feeling of homecoming.

He was saved from any comment by Standish who said, "You're one up on me, Professor. I didn't know who he was. Told him to leave. Sorry about that, Mr. Wyndham. Or is it Lord Wyndham? Us Americans have trouble with that sort of thing."

"Sir James, actually, not that it matters. Professor...?"

"Kristina McGinnis," she replied and curtsied to him. At his startled look, she said, "You'll have to forgive me but we do strive for historical accuracy. That's why we're here."

"Is it? I'm not clear on what this is all about, Professor. Suppose you explain it."

His tone was matter-of-fact but with an inflection of command that no one could mistake. He was a man used to being in charge and accustomed to others doing as he told them. Four years of captivity had not changed that.

Standish looked surprised, but Kristina took the order in stride. She handed the spoon to the younger man. "Keep stirring, Francis. The porridge should be done in a few minutes and there's a rasher of bacon you can slice. Perhaps Sir James will join us for breakfast."

"Perhaps," James said noncommittally. "First a few answers, if you please, Professor."

She wiped her hands on a length of cloth hung on a metal peg to the side of the fireplace and gestured toward the door. "I can do better than that, Sir James. How about the quarter tour?"

Her good humor had what was undoubtedly the desired effect. He relaxed slightly and nodded. "Lead on."

Outside in the bailey, the light had grown stronger. Kristina stood for a moment, letting her eyes adjust. She took a deep breath and said softly, "I love the smell of this place, the wood smoke and old stones, the heather and the sea. There's nothing else quite like it."

"You're American," James observed. "The enthusiasm is a dead giveaway."

"Is that what does it?" she asked teasingly. "I thought it was our tendency to butcher the English language."

"That, too. What are you a professor of?"

"Medieval history. I teach at Harvard University."

He was impressed despite himself. Kristina McGinnis might be a charming nut, but her credentials were heavy duty. "Why aren't you there now?"

"I received a grant from the University and the British government to study thirteenth-century living conditions in situ. That means we don't just prowl through old documents or try to dig up artifacts, we actually live as people did back then."

"To what purpose?"

"Greater knowledge and understanding of the time. The thirteenth century was an important period. Major advances were made in technology and agriculture that improved the standard of living for everyone, extended the life span and caused a big jump in the population. We want to know how people coped, what they did that was right and what they did that was wrong."

"Do you really have to go in for all this playacting in order to accomplish that?" James asked skeptically.

Kristina shrugged. The question failed to offend her. He suspected she had dealt with it often enough before. "Waking up freezing cold because you forgot to keep the fire going and having to spend an hour getting it started again drives home what daily life was like for these people more effectively than hours in the classroom. We eat the same foods they did, we work with the same tools, we face many of the same problems. By the time we finish here, my students will have an understanding of the period that they could not possibly get in any other way. They'll be better scholars and, I like to think, better people. Certainly, they won't be so inclined to take the fabric of their own lives for granted."

She stopped and looked at him apologetically. "I'm sorry, I tend to start lecturing at the drop of a hat. Even worse, I can go on about Innishffarin for hours. Suppose I just show you instead?"

He agreed and followed her as they crossed the bailey. Kristina pointed out the forge that had been reopened in its original location and was once again fully operational. "We're not producing weapons or armor," she assured him, "but our smithy, Jergus, has become very proficient at ax heads and saws. You'll notice that the baking ovens next door back up directly to the common wall the bakery and forge share. We think that was done in an attempt to conserve heat and make the best possible use of it."

"Very sensible," James murmured. As she moved past him he caught a whiff of honey. Her skin looked smooth and sun-warmed. There was a smattering of freckles across her nose.

"You're really serious about this," he said quietly.

She stopped near the door and looked at him. "Yes, I am. We all are. We were very grateful to your brother, Richard, when he gave permission for us to use the castle, but of course, we're aware that the ultimate decision is yours. I hope you'll agree that we can stay."

James hesitated. Now that he had seen more of what was going on at Innishffarin, it seemed harmless enough. But Kristina McGinnis disturbed him. Without trying to, she reached straight through the shell he had constructed around his emotions and made him aware of himself in a way he did not care to be.

His priority was simple—to return to the life that had always been his. Given the stakes, that would be no easy task. He did not need to be distracted by a woman with sunlit hair, forest eyes, and an imagination in which time could be turned back upon itself.

The past was gone, it could never be recovered no matter what Kristina McGinnis thought. Only the present was real.

And yet, he needed no great imagination to see the hurt that would appear in her green-gold eyes if he told her the foolishness had to end. Four years of captivity had, if nothing else, made him more sensitive to the pain of others and more reluctant to cause it.

"All right," he said suddenly before he could reconsider, "you can stay." In the back of his mind was the thought that it made no difference; he rarely came to Innishffarin and would have no reason to see her again.

He pushed the regret he felt at that aside with the same ruthlessness he had come to depend on while a prisoner. Yet he lingered another hour at Innish-ffarin, breakfasting on porridge, bacon, thick brown bread and cheese washed down by milk. The food was delicious and the company of the students, who were all at least as enthusiastic as their professor, was amusing.

He told himself that was why he paused twice on the ridge above the castle and looked back at the ancient stones coming alive again in the sun.

Chapter 2

Kristina frowned as she bent over the faint tracings of ink on the page in front of her. Despite the sunlight streaming in through the chapel windows, it was difficult to make out the writing. She shifted slightly, trying to find a more comfortable position.

The book carefully balanced on her knees was large, about a foot high and almost as wide with a thickness of several inches. The leather covering was elaborately etched and engraved with gold. Inside, the vellum folios were illustrated with graceful pen and ink drawings. Although the colors had faded over the centuries, it was still possible to see that a skilled artist had been at work.

The book was the account of a journey to Scotland taken by one Linus Woolsthorpe, a merchant adventurer who left the relative comforts of London for a year in the Highlands. Why he would have done so baffled Kristina for Linus had clearly not been a happy camper.

Through the several hundred pages of his manuscript, he complained constantly about the wildness and savagery of the place, the roughness of the people and the lack of even the most basic creature comforts.

He caught cold several times and described the resulting symptoms in tireless detail, got lost repeatedly because he seemed to possess no sense of direction whatsoever, fired his servants or had them wander off, and generally had a miserable time of it.

Yet he persevered and eventually he came to Innishffarin. There his eye for detail did not desert him. He described the castle down to practically the last stone, even including numerous sketches of it.

Although properly wary of the laird—who sounded as though he weren't all that different from the present one—Linus had stayed on for more than a month. He found much to complain about but his heart didn't seem to be in it. Innishffarin impressed him.

Most especially, he was overwhelmed by the great celebration given to honor the Wyndham son who was returning from the Crusade. He described the festivities with loving care beginning with the entry of the son into Innishffarin accompanied by his baggage train containing "several coffers of treasure captured from the infidel."

Kristina rubbed the back of her neck absently, trying without much success to ease the stiffness. She was wasting her time reading Linus again. He had nothing new to tell her and besides, she had virtually memorized all he had to say on the subject of Innishffarin. For all his carping, he had been an accurate reporter. Everything she had learned since beginning work at the castle indicated that.

The question was whether he was accurate enough. "Several coffers of treasure" and yet only the Byzantine cross now in the chapel had ever been found. So far as the Wyndhams were concerned, it seemed to be enough. They were convinced there was nothing more to find.

Richard Wyndham made that quite clear when Kristina broached the subject with him during their first meeting. But she remained unconvinced. If Linus was right, Sir Reginald Wyndham had brought back a trove of early medieval manuscripts, reliquaries, jewelry, and other valuables that might still be hidden somewhere within the castle grounds. She meant to find them.

But at the moment she had milk to churn. With a sigh, she put the book away and went back outside. A quick glance around assured her that everything was proceeding smoothly. Two of her students were working with simple awls and axes to build a plow of the sort no one had seriously used in a half dozen centuries. Others were busy boiling laundry in a large kettle while nearby several experimented with making lye for soap from wood ash.

At midday they would all meet to compare experiences and discuss the day's topic, nutritional levels among thirteenth-century yeomanry.

Sometime between now and then she had to work up at least a little enthusiasm for the subject. It wasn't fair to her students—or to herself—for her to be wandering around distracted all the time.

"Get a grip, girl," she murmured under her breath as she went into the dairy barn. The cows had been milked and let out to pasture. She could hear them lowing softly as she set to work. As she splashed milk into the wooden churner, she deliberately kept her mind blank. The chore was one she had done dozens of times, she didn't need to think about it or anything else.

Especially not James Wyndham.

A slight flush stained her cheeks as she realized it was happening again. Trying not to think about him only seemed to guarantee that she would do exactly that. He kept cropping up in her thoughts at odd times throughout the day and at night...

Never mind what happened at night. She absolutely would not think about the dreams she kept having. Absolutely not.

Resignedly, she sat down in front of the churner and set to work. If nothing else, medieval living was great for fitness. Who needed aerobics or jogging when they had to do eight or ten hours of manual labor every day? She was in the best shape of her life, as happy as she had ever been and doing the work she loved.

So why the vague sense of discontent that had been growing in her ever since that single, brief meeting with James Wyndham a week before? It was as though he had taken her peace of mind with him when he rode away.

A groan escaped her as she realized that she was thinking about him yet again. Impatiently, she yanked the churner harder than she should have. The pole flew out, landing some distance away in a pile of hay, and the bucket flipped over, sending milk running in rivulets across the dirt floor.

Kristina had an impressive command of both Middle English and Latin. She used them both to blistering effect as she set about cleaning up the mess. By the time she was done she had decided that her problem wasn't James Wyndham, it was herself. She had been holed up at Innishffarin nonstop for two months and she needed a break.

Half an hour later, with a hastily assembled "wish" list from her students in hand, she was walking down the country lane that linked the castle to the village of Innishffarin. The sun was shining, a pleasant breeze blew off the sea, and birds called softly from the flowering heather.

No jets roared overhead, no cars lumbered past. The air was crystal clear and the small brook where she paused for a drink could not have been purer. She could almost believe that even beyond the castle walls, the twentieth-century world did not yet exist.

Until, that is, she rounded a corner and started down the long hill that led to the village. Just as she did so, the peaceful day was shattered by the roar of a powerful sports car. Kristina barely had time to jump to one side as it sped past.

She caught a quick glimpse of a woman behind the wheel, an elegantly angular face framed by a silk scarf and shielded by oversize sun glasses. Then the car was gone in a cloud of acrid exhaust.

Kristina got to her feet, coughing. Angrily, she brushed the dirt and grass from the tunic she still wore and pushed the stray wisps of hair from her eyes. Okay, there were problems in 1292, it was far from a perfect world. But they didn't have maniacs tearing along at 80 mph trying to mow down innocent pedestrians.

Grumbling, she continued on her way and reached the village a few minutes later. The village of Innishffarin was little more than a single main street about a quarter mile in length and framed on either side with modest two-story dwellings, many with the ground floor converted to shops. A few cars were parked along the road but they were outnumbered by bicycles and motorcycles, the preferred means of transport on such a pleasant day.

The exception was the pub, an ancient, rambling building in the Tudor style with an adjoining parking lot that had been a stable yard. Several dozen cars were parked there but Kristina had no trouble spotting the one that had nearly run her down.

Anger surged in her once again but she forced it down. She had better things to do. To begin with, there was the list of small, much-missed items from her students that included everything from sports magazines to chewing gum. While everyone was making a genuine effort to live on thirteenth-century terms, a few small exceptions were good for morale.

Two doors down from the pub was the grocer. Kristina had shopped there several times when she first came to Innishffarin. The plump, motherly woman behind the counter recognized her straight away.

"Why Professor McGinnis," Mary Horliss said, "as I live and breathe, we've all been wondering what's been going on with you lot up at the castle. Thought maybe you'd vanished into the mist like that *Brigadoon* story. Not a day goes by that I don't say to my Harry, imagine living like folks did all those centuries ago. Couldn't do it meself, not without my telly."

"It's not as bad as you think, Mrs. Horliss," Kristina told her. "No telly, that's true, but every evening we appoint someone to be bard and that person leads us in stories and songs. We even have a minstrel although he does think music began and ended with the Beatles. I've learned all the words to 'Eleanor Rigby' and I can almost do 'Yesterday' backwards!''

"Oh, well, as long as you aren't wasting your time. Now what can I do for you, lass? A nice bit of chocolate maybe, or something for your hair? That's an...um...interesting thingamajig you're wearing. I thought the grand ladies wore silks and satins and those funny pointed hats with lovely white veils trailing from them.''

"Alas," Kristina said with a smile, "it's a poor working woman I'm supposed to be. Besides, these clothes are a lot more comfortable.''

"True enough," Mary agreed, "and there's nothing wrong with being a worker. Can't stand a fancy, rich layabout meself." She leaned forward slightly and said, "Believe me, we've seen plenty of them around in the last few years but no more, I'd wager. Not now that the laird's back, praise be. You know about that, do you?''

Kristina nodded and tried to ignore the sudden skip of her pulse. "We're all very glad, of course. Sir James was kind enough to come by the day after he got back.'' She hesitated, knowing that she ought to change the subject, but instead she said, "Not that we've seen him since. I suppose he's busy at the Manor.''

"Oh, he hasn't been there," Mary said. "He went straight off to London. It must have been the same day you saw him. Quite a hoo-ha it's been, him getting control of the business again. Mr. Richard's all bent out of shape but there's nothing he can do about it. After all, he was supposedly just taking care of things until the laird himself could get back." She nodded with satisfaction. "Well, now he is and if you ask me, there's going to be hell to pay. Ought to be a bang-up weekend."

"Why?" Kristina asked, giving up all pretense of being other than intensely interested.

"Because they're all going to be back here," Mary informed her. "Least that's what my sister's girl, Liz, says. And she ought to know seeing as how she helps out at the manor. She says Mr. Richard's already here and Mr. James is expected today for the weekend. And then of course, there's that woman."

Kristina repressed a sigh. She knew she shouldn't ask—and for a moment she even thought she might manage not to—but inevitably the words came out. "What woman?"

"Why Theresa d'Auberville Westerloo, of course. Don't you read the papers? She's always being mentioned in the society columns and they never fail to tell you who she is. 'Fiancée of the industrialist, James Wyndham, held captive in Lebanon.' That's what they always say or did until last week."

Mary rolled her eyes. "Fiancée indeed. If you ask me, she should have spent the last four years doing something to help him instead of gadding about the way she did. Up here in season and always with Mr. Richard. Why, the two of them have been practically inseparable."

"Are you saying..."

Mary laid a finger beside her nose and looked solemn. "Ask me no questions, I'll tell you no lies. But I will say this, some people are no better than they have to be. No better at all."

It was like a soap opera, Kristina thought a short time later as she left the store. The prodigal son returns only to discover that in his absence there have been shenanigans between his brother and his intended. Meanwhile, the locals wait with bated breath for the fireworks to begin.

It might have been amusing if the people hadn't been real and the implications tragic. Surely James Wyndham had suffered enough? The thought that he would have to deal with such perfidy was unpleasant enough without contemplating what his reaction was likely to be.

Standing on the corner near the store, Kristina shivered slightly. The sudden chill she felt had nothing whatsoever to do with the weather, which was almost balmy.

Rather it was related to the inexplicable but nonetheless undeniable sense she had that the laird of Innishffarin was a dangerous man well capable of defending what he regarded as his own, or exacting vengeance against anyone who had trespassed there. Despite herself, she couldn't help but feel a certain sympathy for the hapless pair.

They were still on her mind when she entered the pub, glanced around for a moment and somewhat guiltily found herself a seat in a cubby. The guilt was in anticipation of what she was about to do. It wasn't fair to her students, it was weak, but she simply couldn't help herself.

When the gum-cracking waitress appeared, Kristina looked her straight in the eye and said, "I'd like a pot of tea, please."

Actually, she was just about ready to kill for one but there was no point going into that. It was two months since she'd had a sip of tea, or coffee, or cola, any-thing at all that contained caffeine. Her craving should surely be gone but instead all she had to do was get within a whiff of any of the above and she was over-come. Never mind the guilt, she was going to enjoy every drop.

And she would have if she hadn't happened to lean her head against the back of the cubby just in time to become aware of what the people on the other side were saying. She couldn't see them but the man's voice was definitely familiar, very upper crust British with a hint of weary impatience. The woman's she didn't recognize at all which she surely would have if she'd heard it before since the woman sounded by far the more interesting. It wasn't all that often that she heard someone coming apart at the seams.

"I tell you, I can't go on a moment longer. It's in-human, that's what it is. He's playing with us like a cat—what am I saying, like a tiger—with a mouse. Any moment he'll decide to finish us off." She broke off, apparently unable to go on.

"Easy, Tessa," the man said, more as an order than a plea. He was clearly not in the mood for hysterics. "You have no more idea of what he's thinking than I do. I admit he's wasted no time but everything he's done so far has involved the firm. He hasn't said a word to either of us that was remotely personal."

"And you don't find that terrifying?" Tessa de-manded. "I'm his fiancée, for heaven's sake. He's been away for four years cooped up in some hellhole where he certainly hasn't had any feminine compan-ionship, yet he's been back a week and hasn't come anywhere near me. I'm sorry, but I think that's omi-nous."

"What's the matter, dear heart, can't stand the idea that our James finds your charms infinitely resistible? At this particular moment, I wish to hell that I could say the same thing for myself."

"Bastard," the woman said in a harsh whisper. "None of this was my idea. You took advantage of how confused and frightened I was."

"Bull. We were attracted to each other from the beginning and you know it. If James and your father hadn't been so determined on that grand alliance of Wyndham and Westerloo interests, the engagement would never have happened. When he disappeared in Beirut, we saw our opportunity and took it. It was that simple."

"You make it sound horrible, as though we didn't care about him. But I do, I honestly do, and I wish to God there was some way to convince him."

"Save it," the man said coldly. "James will come to whatever conclusions he likes without any assistance from us and there isn't a damn thing we can do about it."

"We don't have to be here. We could go somewhere..."

"No, he's my brother and I'll face him when I have to. If you've got an ounce of decency, you'll do the same."

"I'm not sure I can Richard. It's all so—"

"Miss, your tea."

Kristina jerked her attention back to the waitress who had reappeared beside her table. The woman seemed to have been trying to get her attention for several seconds with no success. Kristina had been totally absorbed in the conversation going on behind her. Blushing at the extent of her eavesdropping, she shifted uncomfortably on the bench.

"If you don't mind," she said, gesturing to a table at the far end of the room, "I'll have it over there."

When the waitress frowned, Kristina added quickly. "I'd like to look out the window."

As the window in question provided a view of the parking lot, the waitress could be forgiven for finding the request odd. But she went along with it all the same. Kristina breathed a sigh of relief as she left the cubby behind. Tessa—Theresa d'Auberville Wester-loo—and her companion, doubtlessly Richard Wynd-ham, deserved at least some privacy.

But her good intentions turned out to be for nought. Barely had she sat down at the table than she realized that though her new position prevented her from hearing the pair, it now permitted her to see them. Her eyes widened slightly as she discovered that the un-happy Miss Westerloo was also the woman in the speeding sports car. Her concern for herself did not extend to others, if her driving habits were anything to judge by.

Kristina took a sip of her tea but the pleasure was considerably dimmed by what had just happened. She felt as though she had become an interloper in a sad and rather ugly place where she most definitely did not belong. Long before she had intended doing so, she left most of the tea still in the pot and got up from the table.

In the short time she had been inside, the weather had changed. A damp wind blew out of the west and heavy gray clouds obscured the sky. Kristina cast them a worried glance as she set off down the road. She had three miles to go. If she was lucky, she might make it before it started to pour.

She wasn't. Barely had she gotten beyond the village when the heavens opened. The rain was cold and dank. It slid down the back of her tunic, sloshed through her sandals and turned the road to mud.

Thoroughly uncomfortable and not a little disgusted, Kristina pressed on doggedly. She had no choice. The road wound along close to the cliffs above the sea. There was no shelter, not even a decent-size tree. The best she could hope for was to reach the castle before pneumonia set in.

Preoccupied with her misery, Kristina did not notice the horse until it was almost upon her. Unlike the sports car, it came at a polite trot and slowed perceptibly as it neared. From high on the gray horse's back, James surveyed her waterlogged appearance. He thought she looked like a half-drowned nymph but resisted saying so. Instead, he merely smiled and held out his hand.

"Want a lift?"

Chapter 3

Rain lashed the windows like rough, angry fingers trying to pry their way inside. Beyond the panes of leaded glass, the day had turned a dull, sodden gray. The weather was made for misery—chills, sniffles, sinus headaches, and general self-pity. But on the other side of the windows—bliss.

A log plopped as flames danced in the marble-mantled fireplace. Kristina stirred under the cashmere throw that covered her from her chin to her toes. She was sitting in a large wing chair with her feet on an ottoman in front of the fire.

While her own clothes dried, she was sedately garbed in an oversize terry cloth robe that reached clear to her ankles with the sleeves flopped over her hands unless she remembered to keep them rolled up. She had towel dried her hair and left it hanging in a slightly damp, pale gold curtain over her shoulders.

She sighed and shifted in the chair, fighting to keep her eyes open. Her thoughts were a confused jumble of images and sensations backlit by conflicting emotions.

The memory of riding perched high on the huge stallion, held close with James's steely arm wrapped around her waist and his thighs pressing intimately against her own disturbed her. She enjoyed it far too much and slipped back into it far too readily.

She should have insisted that he drop her off at the castle but the manor had actually been closer and the thought of hot, running water and possibly even central heating had overwhelmed her. She had succumbed to temptation with barely a whimper.

And now here she was, stretched out in front of the fire like a contented cat without a care or a responsibility in the world. It was really too shameful.

Of course, there had been that mention of tea. Just before he went off to change his own clothes, James had said something about it. In fact, he had gone further and rung for it, an intriguing process Kristina had heard about often enough but never actually witnessed.

To her disappointment, there was no tasseled velvet cord to pull, only a discreet button embedded in the wall molding which, when pressed, caused the appearance of a gentleman in a dark suit who listened gravely to what was required before vanishing as efficiently as the Cheshire cat.

James had excused himself immediately thereafter and had not yet returned. In the stillness of the big but gracefully proportioned room, Kristina was torn between drowsiness and curiosity.

It was the first time she had been inside the manor, her meetings with Richard having taken place at the London headquarters of Wyndham Industries. She had seen it from afar but that had not prepared her for the sheer size and opulence of the interior.

She smiled as she remembered the old joke: How do you get a beautiful English lawn? Easy, just seed, water and roll for three hundred years.

It was the same here. Several centuries of accumulated wealth and power definitely resulted in some nice architecture. If she hadn't been so relaxed, she might have felt inspired to explore it further. But as it was, she was content to remain curled up in the chair in front of the fire, listening to the snap, crackle, pop of the logs.

In another moment, she would get up, get herself organized, perhaps go check if her clothes were dry providing, of course, that she could find her way back through the maze of hallways and stairs to the guest-room she had used. If she looked hard enough she might find one of those helpful maps of the kind put up on walls of hotels—with a red dot marked You Are Here.

Or perhaps there would be the White Rabbit *tsking* over his pocket watch and forever beckoning her on. Why not, when she already felt more than a little like Alice in Wonderland?

On such thoughts, she drifted until the thoughts turned to dreams, and snuggled comfortably in front of the fire, she slept.

Like a child, James thought, as he walked into the room and discovered her lost in slumber. Hard on the notion came another—that he was a damn fool.

If there was one thing Professor Kristina McGinnis most certainly was not, it was a child. She was an interloper in his life, a disturbing influence, a *Distraction* deserving of a capital *D*. In short, a woman but one unlike any he had ever met before.

Without taking his eyes from her, he sat down in a nearby chair and watched her as she slept. There were faint purple shadows under her eyes and he could see a bruise on the small hand that peered out from beneath the afghan.

Irrational anger flowed through him at the thought of how hard she must be driving herself and for what? Some misbegotten urge to recapture the past in order to better understand it? So far as he was concerned, the past deserved to be forgotten. He was interested only in the future.

But first, he reminded himself, there was the present to deal with.

In the hellhole of Beirut, he had learned one valuable lesson, a small, shining kernel of redemption to take with him out of all the pain and horror: When all was said and done, truth was the only weapon that really counted.

He had learned to cling to truth in the darkness and the despair, to hold fast to who and what he was, a man of courage and of honor, a decent man who did not deserve what was happening to him and who refused to be crushed by it.

Truth had saved him and in the saving, he had come to see it as essential to him as food or water.

Whatever the cost, he would have the truth. Anything that made him forget that for even a moment was a luxury he could not afford. Anything, including a woman with hair like gold and eyes as beckoning as the summer-born forest.

In her sleep, Kristina stirred uneasily. She snuggled farther down in the chair, drawing the afghan with her, but found no comfort there. Something was drawing her back out of dreams into reality, into the centuries-old manor built of ruthless pride and power, where the fire leapt high, into—

She opened her eyes suddenly. James was watching her. For an instant, he appeared to her as though carved from stone, locked within himself, unreachable and unmovable. The impression, fleeting as it was, was frightening. This was a man who set his own course and who, once set on it, would not be moved by heaven or earth. Not a man to be crossed.

And then he smiled just as he had in the instant before he lifted her onto the horse, a smile so real that she could not resist it.

"Are you hungry?" he asked.

"Starved," she admitted.

"Good. Bernie outdid himself."

"Who," Kristina asked as she struggled upright in the chair, "is Bernie?"

"The butler."

Her eyes widened. "You're kidding? Your butler's name is Bernie?"

"What's wrong with that?" James inquired, the smile deepening until it almost, but not quite, reached his eyes.

"Butlers are supposed to be named Smathers or Smithers or something like that."

"I had a dentist once named Smathers but never a butler. Bernie is from Brooklyn originally. I've never been precisely clear on how he ended up as a butler but he does the job well enough and he's been with us for ages. Tea?"

Belatedly, Kristina noticed the tray that had appeared on the table between them as she slept. She nodded. "What's Bernie's last name?"

"Berkowitz. His wife's name is Barbara and they are parents to Bobby, Belinda and Beatrice Berkowitz, all of whom grew up here but have since gone on to other things. Bobby, for instance, is a champion backgammon player. Took the tournament in Monaco last year, which was no surprise. I've been trounced by him myself more times than I care to remember. One lump or two?"

"Lemon, please. What do Belinda and Beatrice do?"

"Belinda looks after twins which is, apparently, a full-time job-and-a-half, while Beatrice is an editor for *Queen* in London."

"How did they manage to escape the family *B* curse?" Kristina inquired. Any moment now the Cheshire cat would be back and the White Rabbit, too, no doubt.

"They didn't," James said as he held out a plate for her inspection. "Belinda married Bannacort Ballentyre, decent enough chap but that made her Belinda Berkowitz Ballentyre which at the very least makes the monogram on the china rather dull. Sandwich?"

"Thanks. What about Beatrice?"

"Still single but Bernie has hopes. She recently met a fellow named Brendan Blodworth who comes from Boston and she seems quite taken with him."

Bemusedly, Kristina accepted a wafer thin sliver of potted salmon nestled between transparent slices of home-baked bread. It melted on her tongue, managing in the brief transition to her stomach to evoke images of rock-strewn rapids, leaping fish, speckled sunlight, and the indescribably satisfying whish of line playing out in the perfect cast. Not bad for a sandwich too small to keep a gnat alive.

"I'll hope for the best for Brendan and Beatrice," she said solemnly. "Any more *B*s lurking about?"

"I think that's it." He got up to toss another log on the fire and give it a poke. Both perfectly normal, even mundane activities. Thousands of people did them every day, especially on dank, rain-swept days.

There was, therefore, no reason to notice how the muscles of his back moved under the plain white cotton shirt he wore, or that the corduroy slacks he had changed into fit him rather well, or that the hand holding the poker was hard with sinew. No reason at all.

Kristina took another sandwich and ate it without tasting. She must be coming down with something. Her head felt stuffed with odd, stray bits of thoughts, ineffable desires, half-formed longings. All the effluvia she usually managed to ignore in her busy, purposeful life.

But not now and not here, high on a hillside in Scotland, wrapped round with elegance and luxury, pampered, cosseted, and feeling for all the world like gossamer thin crystal that might shatter at any moment.

"I should be getting back," she said on a thread of sound.

"Wait until the rain lets up," James suggested—or was it ordered? He was clearly accustomed to command. What must it have meant for a man like that to be suddenly a prisoner, shorn of all control and subject to the whim of captors who would have found pleasure in tormenting him?

Kristina flinched. She put her teacup down too quickly. It slipped along the edge of the table and would have fallen to the floor if James hadn't caught her hand, steadying it.

His eyes met hers, staring right past all her defenses. "What's wrong?"

She shook her head. "Nothing. I'm just tired."

"Nonsense, you're white as a sheet. Are you ill?"

"No...I..." She hesitated, torn between truth and prudence. Truth won as it always seemed to with her, no matter what the consequences.

"My father was a POW in Vietnam. I don't remember him at all from before he went over there, I only know how he was when he finally came home. He's a strong man and a brave one, but the effects were still very hard to deal with."

James stiffened. He pulled away from her and stood up again. His face was blank. "So you've been wondering how I'm faring."

He made it sound like a failing on her part but she refused to accept that. Without apology, she said, "Most of us can't begin to imagine what captivity means. We take so much freedom for granted that when it's suddenly removed from us, we have to find an entirely new way of looking at ourselves and the world. It's impossible to come through an experience like that without being greatly changed. The biggest challenge my father faced when he came home was to accept that he was in many ways a different person."

"Perhaps he was," James said, "but I assure you, I am not. In fact, there are more than a few people in

London who after this last week would bet the home farm on the fact that I'm the same man I always was.''

"They'd be wrong.''

"That's your opinion.''

His tone was cutting and the look in his eyes could have sliced through steel. It this was his manner in the boardroom, Kristina thought, no wonder people were so reluctant to cross him.

And no wonder his brother and fiancée were so afraid of what he might do to them.

Did he know about that at all? Did he have an inkling of what had gone on while he was away? Did he care?

She had no answers and James wasn't about to provide them. He had closed himself off from her. That hurt more than she wanted to admit but she didn't regret her frankness. If her guess was right, everyone else would be tiptoeing around him, hoping to avoid his wrath.

Maybe she ought to be, too, especially since her continued presence at Innishffarin depended on his goodwill. But she couldn't bring herself to pretend that she didn't care about what he was going through.

She did care, a great deal more than was good for her. And because she cared, she wanted him to know that he wasn't alone.

Sleep-rumpled still, her cheeks flushed, she stood up and went to him. The oversize robe covered her completely. Her hair fell in disarray around her shoulders. Barefoot under the robe and several inches shorter than him, she had to tilt her head back to look him in the eye.

Softly, she said, "Do yourself a favor, Sir James. Admit that you're a human being. It's not such a bad thing to be. You might even find that you like it."

He stared at her for what seemed like a long time but was really only seconds. Slowly, almost imperceptibly, the corners of his mouth lifted. But the chill never left his eyes.

"Be careful what you ask for, Kristina McGinnis. You just might get it."

His hands were firm on her shoulders, the lean fingers closing around delicate bones. Belatedly, she was aware of the heat of his body, the sheer size and strength of him making her feel shockingly vulnerable. She had a sudden sense of forces held only precariously in check and then she knew nothing at all.

Nothing except the touch and taste of him, the strength and need, the sheer male power. His kiss was long, hard, demanding. He did not coax or ask, he took. And she—quiet, scholarly Kristina McGinnis— matched him all the way.

It was she who stood on tiptoe to twine her fingers in his thick ebony hair and hold him even closer. She who met the quicksilver thrust of his tongue with a moan of sheer, unfettered delight that sent a tremor through him. And she who, when he tore his mouth from hers to stare questioningly into her eyes, touched his lips with her own in a kiss so gentle as to be a healing balm.

Infinite possibilities swirled around them. They were alone, armored against the world, and caught by forces neither had anticipated or could control. Limits were evaporating, restrictions vanishing. All things could be.

Until the double doors at the far end of the room swung open and a woman's gasp echoed through the room.

Chapter 4

Bernard Berkowitz, being the perfect butler, promptly made himself invisible—a feat that Kristina could not help thinking would have turned the Cheshire cat chartreuse with envy.

The other two were not so fortunate. They stood, frozen in place, eyes wide and mouths agape, the perfect foil for James's icy disdain.

"As usual your timing is perfect. It's uncanny, really, how you manage it."

"Years of practice," Richard said deadpan. "Professor McGinnis, nice to see you again."

"You know her?" Tessa demanded. She stood, fashionably slender to the point of thinness, pale and trembling. Her hands clenched as she looked from one to the other.

Shrilly, she demanded. "James, what is the meaning of this? Why is this woman here and why is she dressed like that?"

He made a small but cutting gesture of impatience and ignored her. Turning to Richard, he said, "You're early."

His brother moved over to a sideboard where several crystal decanters were set out. He poured himself a generous measure of brandy and drank most of it in a single swallow before he answered.

"Only slightly. You did say we might come, or have you forgotten?"

James's smile was chilling. "I rarely forget anything and I've had four years to improve my memory. It's amazing what long, uninterrupted stretches of solitude will do for a man."

Richard threw back his head and finished the brandy. He set the goblet on the sideboard with an audible *clink*. His mouth twisted and his eyes were bleak. Kristina felt a spurt of sympathy for him.

"I'm sure it is," he said. "But you were always the strong one, weren't you? Ruthless, indomitable James, the natural leader of the family. You left them reeling in London, you know. The few executives you deigned to keep in place are thanking their gods while the others ... Ah, well, who cares about them? We're all disposable, aren't we?"

There was a hint of self-pity in his words that made Kristina fear what James's response would be. She doubted he had much tolerance for that sort of thing. He surprised her.

Quietly, he said, "No, we're not. I learned that the hard way. You look a wreck. Go and lie down for a while."

Richard laughed, a little shakily. "I hear and obey. Actually, I think I'll just have a hot soak." He gave

Kristina a surprisingly jaunty smile. "See you later, Professor McGinnis?"

"No," she said quickly. "Actually, I'll be heading back to the castle."

"Don't let us run you off," Tessa chimed in. When it came to smiles, she had a shark beat six ways to Sunday.

Kristina resisted the impulse to count her fingers and headed for the door. "I'll just get my clothes."

Tessa wasn't done yet, or maybe she was just nervous. Either way, she felt compelled to get in one more dig. "You do remember where you left them?"

"It'll come to me," Kristina muttered. She was out of there. Not for nothing had she spent a good part of her life avoiding exactly this kind of messy entanglement. Give her the good old slash-and-burn world of academe. She knew her way around there. Upper crust drawing room intrigues were beyond her.

So was finding her clothes. After stumbling around in the upper reaches of the manor for several minutes, she finally located the room she had used. Her only thought was to get dressed. She'd figure out how to get back to Innishffarin once she'd accomplished that.

But it wasn't so simple. Her clothes were nowhere to be found. She had left them hung neatly over the brass towel warmer in the hope that they would dry more quickly. Now the warmer held only a collection of white, fluffy towels emblazoned with the Wyndham crest.

Exasperated, she sat down on the edge of the high, four-poster bed and tried to decide what to do. Her brief nap had still left her tired and the scene in the drawing room hadn't helped. She felt dazed, perplexed and ineffably sad. It was all she could do not to curl up on the big bed, pull the fur throw at the bottom of it up over her, and let sleep claim her.

Rather than give in to the temptation, she forced herself back onto her feet. Clearly, her clothes had to be somewhere. All she had to do was track them down.

But before she could do that, there was a knock at the bedroom door. Hesitantly, she opened it, hoping not to find Tessa on the other side. Her wish was granted. There was no sign of the angry Miss Westerloo. Instead, a young maid stood there holding a shimmering white gown draped over her arm.

"Afternoon miss. If you please, I've brought your dress."

Kristina's instant relief faded as she glanced at the garment. It looked as though it had been spun from cobwebs and stardust. There could hardly have been a greater contrast to the sensible and rather primitive garb she had worn.

"That isn't mine," she said, not without a note of regret for the gown looked impossibly beautiful.

"Oh, I know, miss," the maid said with a smile. She moved lightly into the room and laid the dress carefully on the bed. "It belongs to Miss Jillian but his lordship said he thought it would fit you. I brought the necessaries as well," she added, indicating a pile of fragile lingerie and the delicate slippers she had also carried.

"Oh, he did, did he?" Kristina muttered. Of all the high-handed, presumptuous... He knew she was leaving. She had said so quite clearly. Yet he ignored that and intended what? That she stay, obviously, and further that she play the willing guest even to rigging herself out in a dress that looked as though it was held together by good intentions and very little else.

"Who," she asked tautly, "is Miss Jillian?"

"Why Mr. James's and Mr. Richard's sister, miss. She lives in New York now, works as a model, she does." The maid's eyes grew dreamy. "Has the most marvelous taste in clothes. You ought to see some of the other things she left here. But this is the best, I have to say. It will go wonderfully with your coloring."

"It will go period," Kristina said. "I'd like my own clothes, please. I'm leaving."

The maid looked shocked. "You can't do that, miss. The laird expects you at dinner."

"Then *the laird* is hard of hearing." At the maid's shocked look, Kristina relented slightly. He was, after all, her host. "I don't mean to be rude, Miss...?"

"Megan, and it's just that there must be some misunderstanding. It's terrible weather, it is, and the road back to Innishffarin will be inches deep in mud. Why would you want to go there, anyway, when you can stay here till morning?"

A cajoling note crept into Megan's voice as she eyed Kristina encouragingly. "I'm sure his lordship will take you back himself as soon as the weather clears but for right now, the sensible thing is for you to stay. And if you have to stay anyway, well, then, you'll be wanting dinner, won't you?"

"On a tray," Kristina suggested weakly, "here?" She had a sudden and most unsettling sense of being steamrollered. Megan might look like a stiff breeze would blow her away but when it came to watching out for the interests of her employer, she didn't take no for an answer.

Megan's eyes twinkled. She bustled about, laying a brush, comb, and other implements on the Queen Anne dressing table. Her eyes twinkled. "Now that wouldn't be hospitable, not when there's the whole grand dining hall and the best plate being brought out tonight in honor of the laird being home. I'm sure you don't want to miss it."

And that, it seemed, was that. Short of being an absolutely dreadful guest and terrible ingrate, Kristina had no choice but to play along. To be honest, she wasn't as reluctant as she tried to seem. She had a normal dose of curiosity and probably a bit extra.

What exactly would happen when *the laird* sat down at the table with his brother and the wayward Tessa? And why should she be invited—no, compelled—to join them? The thought flitted through her mind that James was being deliberately provocative. He might know more about Richard and Tessa than he had so far revealed, and he might find the idea of an "extra" woman, particularly one he'd been caught kissing, an amusing addition to the evening.

But she'd be damned if he'd stir the pot at her expense. Never mind the instinctive sympathy she felt for him or that he provoked other, even stronger emotions. She was a stranger, an outsider, and strictly an observer. Nothing was going to involve her in the problems of the tumultuous Wyndham clan. Absolutely nothing.

Or so she told herself as she stepped gingerly into the Hall, very capital *H* as in Great Hall, seat of the lairds of Wyndham since back when the manor was first built and unmistakably a place for holding court. The shimmering white gown shone starkly against the darkness of the oak-paneled walls.

To her great relief, the dress was deceptive. It looked like gossamer because of the way it reflected light but was actually far more modest. It even fit her fairly well except through the bust where Miss Jillian was apparently slightly less amply endowed. She tugged at the neckline, took a deep breath and stepped into the room.

The others were already there. James stood by the fireplace, smoking a cheroot and looking devastating in starkly black evening dress. Richard was more classically handsome in the men's fashion magazine mode, but beside his brother he looked more a boy than a man.

Perhaps that was uncharitable. James would have overwhelmed virtually anyone. Nearby, Tessa sat on the edge of a brocade couch, looking brittle in a bright red sequined gown that should have been tawdry but instead was the last word in elegance. She had the figure for it, Kristina acknowledged, and the presence. Had it not been for the frown marring her smooth brow, she would have been perfect.

The look she gave Kristina would have cut a block of ice but it failed to have the desired effect. Instead, Kristina nodded to the men, smiled at Tessa and deliberately sat down near her.

"I don't believe we've met," she said, extending her hand. "I'm Kristina McGinnis."

Tessa was surprised but she rebounded quickly and offered her own hand. In her cool, modulated voice she said, "Tessa Westerloo. Lovely dress, Miss McGinnis."

"Actually, it belongs to Jillian Wyndham. I'm just borrowing it. My own clothes got soaked in the rain and anyway, they aren't quite in keeping with the occasion."

"I don't know about that, Professor," Richard said. "Dinner in the Great Hall with the laird? Surely, a little something from the thirteenth century wouldn't be totally inappropriate?"

"Only if I was serving dinner," Kristina replied with a smile, "not sitting down to it."

"I don't understand," Tessa said. She looked from one to the other, baffled. "What's the thirteenth century got to do with anything?"

Richard laughed and came over to join them. He looked a bit more relaxed than he had at first, as though he had made up his mind to try to have a good time no matter what.

"The professor will tell you it has a great deal to do. We are the products of our past, don't you agree, James?"

Wyndham's laird tossed the remains of the cheroot into the fireplace and came to join them. The play of light and shadow over his face made his features appear as though carved from stone. There was a deep silence within him that effectively hid his thoughts.

"Only up to a point," he said as he sat down on the couch next to Kristina. She caught the faint scent of tobacco and soap mingling with a subtle aftershave she could not identify. Determinedly, she shut her mind to the sudden influx of emotion that threatened to overwhelm her.

Above them, the ceiling soared a full three stories. Earlier, she had thought the drawing room palatial but the Great Hall put it to shame. It ran the entire length of one wing of the manor. The plastered walls were divided by ornamental moldings framing immense canvases any museum would have gladly claimed. In between them were what appeared to be ancient battle flags tattered and singed but still hanging proudly.

At either end of the Hall were two huge fireplaces topped by flagstone chimneys. Around one was the seating area furnished, as was much of the rest of the house, in the Queen Anne style, at once elegant but comfortable. On the other side of the room stood a pedestal-mounted dining table of gold-hued oak framed by two dozen high-backed chairs. At each place, crystal, china and heavy silver gleamed in the flickering light of candelabra.

Kristina resisted the impulse to ask who else was joining them and gave her attention to Richard.

He was explaining to Tessa about the experiment underway at Innishffarin. Or at least he was trying to. She seemed bewildered as to why anyone would contemplate such a thing.

"Isn't it awfully uncomfortable?" she asked.

"It can be," Kristina admitted. "To be honest, that's why we chose this time of year. None of us felt up to roughing it through a Scotch winter."

"They are dreadful," Tessa agreed. She shivered delicately.

Kristina doubted that would be the case in the snug comfort of Wyndham but she didn't say so. Instead, she accepted a sherry from Richard and sat back to watch the other three.

The tension in the room was palpable yet James seemed oblivious to it. If he was aware of the discomfort his brother and fiancée experienced, he showed no sign of it. They might have gathered for a simple, at-home dinner; friends and acquaintances, enjoying themselves on an inclement night.

In a way, Kristina decided, the pretense was cruel. James seemed almost to be toying with Tessa and Richard, and for that matter with herself, whose attendance at this little get-together he had so imperiously arranged.

She took a sip of the sherry, found it excellent and decided that she wasn't going to play along, at least not entirely. She hadn't known James Wyndham very long but she was already certain that it wasn't a good idea to always let him have his own way.

Deliberately, she said, "I owe you an apology, Miss Westerloo, and if you don't mind, I'd just as soon get it out of the way now."

Tessa narrowed her rather spectacular sapphire eyes. "Whatever do you mean?"

"I'm aware that before Sir James was kidnapped, you and he were engaged. I wouldn't want you to think that I just presumed that relationship no longer existed. What you saw in the drawing room was unplanned and—" she broke off for a moment and looked directly at James "—unfortunate."

Tessa cleared her throat. She smiled nervously. "You're very blunt, Professor." She used Kristina's academic title as though it might somehow explain her remarkable candor. Something had to.

Kristina shrugged. "You're all in a rather difficult situation. I just wouldn't want to add to it, that's all."

Richard laughed. His response was sudden and without pretense. He shook his head in admiration. "Difficult, Professor? Why would you say that? My brother has come back from Lebanon convinced that someone close to him—possibly me—deliberately arranged his kidnapping. He's kept everyone at arm's length and more since his return. Everyone, that is, except you. He refuses to say anything about what he's thinking or feeling. You find that difficult?''

"I find it curiously familiar," Kristina said quietly.

"Professor McGinnis's father was a POW in Vietnam," James interjected. "She had all sorts of theories about my psychological state."

"I wouldn't mind hearing them," Richard said.

James snorted and was about to say what he thought of that when Kristina cut in.

"That isn't what I was referring to. The story is familiar because it has to do with something that happened in your family before. This isn't the first time a Wyndham son has come home after a long absence to quarrel with his brother. The last time it cost you all very dearly."

"She's talking about Sir Reginald," Richard said. "You do take the bull by the horns, don't you, Professor?"

Tessa was getting tired of not understanding what was being said. With asperity, she demanded, "Who was Sir Reginald?"

"A younger son of the family back in the twelfth century," James replied. He spoke without looking at her. His eyes were fixed on Kristina. Quietly, he continued, "He went off to the Crusade to seek his fortune. After many years, he returned. There was a falling out between him and his elder brother. The conflict led to violence and both were killed."

"What did they fight over?" Tessa asked.

James hesitated. He was clearly waiting to see if Kristina would answer. When she did not, he shrugged, "Who knows? It was all a very long time ago. Bernie seems ready to serve. Shall we?"

Kristina had never before sat down to dine in such sumptuous circumstances with so few people. She thought it would be awkward but the other three seemed well accustomed to it. Certainly, James showed no sign of discomfort as he took his place at the head of the table. Tessa and Richard sat on either side of him with Kristina next to Richard.

Although the food was delicious and the service impeccable, Tessa ate little. Kristina's early resort to honesty had apparently convinced her that they could be in for an evening of actual truths. That was enough to put her off her appetite.

Richard was similarly afflicted. He drank a great deal of wine and generally ignored what was on his plate. This despite the fact that James allowed no turn of the conversation into what any of them might think of as dangerous waters.

Instead, he used Kristina shamelessly as a diversion. He got her to talk about Innishffarin and he kept her talking while the salmon grew warm and the filet chilled, until she almost felt like asking if she would also be compelled to sing for her supper.

Not that she minded entirely. She was, after all, an historian and a scholar. She loved to talk about her work. She just wished she could do it under more congenial circumstances.

Dessert arrived as she was explaining the design of the castle's drainage system. Tessa was glassy-eyed. Richard roused himself to ask for the port. Both seemed worn down. Only James appeared hale and hearty.

Far too much of both in Kristina's estimate. Even as she discussed weight loads on stone arches, she was remembering the feel of his mouth against hers, the overwhelming strength of his arms, and the driving need he unleashed within her.

And they only shared a kiss. What would happen—heaven help her—if they ever went further?

Not that they would, she told herself hastily. Absolutely not. As she had assured Tessa, what had happened was unplanned and unfortunate. It was a fluke, an aberration, a once-in-a-blue-moon leap into the dark that would never be repeated.

"Tea, miss?" Butler Berkowitz inquired as he bent over her solicitously. Her hands were trembling slightly. She hid them in her lap and nodded.

"Please."

It was only as he poured that she happened to look up through the high French windows out into the garden. Moonlight fell over the formal beds and gravel paths. It sparkled off the water in the fountain where carp slept.

The rain had stopped. She could return to Innishffarin.

Chapter 5

James agreed to drive her back. He waited while she shucked the borrowed gown and put on her own clothes. They'd been drying in the kitchen where, Butler Berkowitz let it be known, they had been treated with respectful curiosity.

Ready to go, Kristina looked around for Tessa and Richard to say good-night but they had both disappeared. With all the rooms in the manor, they could be anywhere. She thought of the conversation she had overheard in the pub and wondered if they were together. Then she wondered if that had occurred to James.

If it had, he gave no sign of it as he met her at the front doors. He was still dressed in his evening clothes but had removed the tie and loosened the top button of his shirt. The informality suited him. He looked less intimidating than he had before, with a hint of roguishness that was undeniably attractive.

"It's turned into a nice night," he said as they walked down the half dozen steps together.

A few stray clouds skittered across the moon but the air was clear and almost balmy. She smelled the sea mingling with the scent of pine and night-drowsing heather. The unease that had plagued her all evening slipped away. She felt suddenly lighter, as though her feet were no longer so firmly rooted to the ground but drifted instead in some faerie-conjured mist.

He drove a beat-up Range Rover that had seen better days—a decade or so ago. Kristina was surprised. She had guessed him for a Jaguar man or perhaps a Porsche. When she said as much, he laughed.

"I had a Jaguar years back. Damned electrical system never worked right."

"I heard they fixed that finally."

He nodded. "I heard that, too, but it was too late for me."

"How do you mean?"

"Guess I'd grown up by then. Anyway, you may have noticed the roads around here aren't the fanciest. They chew up anything that isn't four-wheel drive."

"Just like home," she said with a smile. "Although we've got hills, not highlands, and the scenery isn't quite so spectacular."

He shot her a quick glance. By moonlight, his eyes looked more silver than blue. Deeply set and thickly fringed, they revealed nothing. Nothing, that is, except the power behind them, the unrelenting strength and proudly fierce will.

Having spent more time with him now, she better understood Tessa's fear. She, too, would not want to be a woman who had betrayed James Wyndham.

When he turned his attention back to the road, she relaxed slightly, glad that he could not know her thoughts.

"Where is home?" he asked.

"Northeastern Connecticut. My parents ran a sports fishing operation. We lived in the back of beyond but I loved it."

"Not a city girl," he observed.

She shook her head. "I can't say I am although I did get to like London while I was studying there."

"'When a man is tired of London he is tired of life,'" he quoted. "It's true, you know. I used to keep myself busy by taking imaginary walks through the city, trying to remember exactly what was along each street or around each corner. By now, I'm probably fully qualified to drive a cab."

His willingness to say anything at all related to how he had spent the years of his captivity surprised Kristina. She was also relieved by it. That he could actually make a joke about that terrible time was the best sign possible that he was getting over it.

"Oh, I don't know," she teased. "I thought London cab drivers had to be able to do a lot more than that. Save lives, deliver babies, perform miracles, solve the mysteries of life, that sort of thing."

"True," James said deadpan. "Maybe it's just as well I've got something else to fall back on."

They drove in silence for a few minutes, watching the moon reflected in the surging sea. The sound of breakers on the rocky shore and the murmur of the wind all but drowned out the muted sounds of the car. They were wrapped in night, enveloped in stillness. The turbulent world might not have existed. But it did and neither of them could forget it.

Quietly, James said, "You were very nice to Tessa. Not, mind you, that she necessarily appreciates it. Candor isn't her strong suit."

"I owed her an apology," Kristina insisted. She really didn't want to discuss the kiss they had shared. It was bad enough that she couldn't stop thinking about it.

"Actually, you didn't."

Her eyebrows rose. "I'm sorry but I don't see how you can say that. You and she are engaged."

"Were," he corrected gently. "We decided to get married a few months before I left for Lebanon. To be blunt, it was a business arrangement that suited us both at the time. But four years have passed and a hell of a lot has changed. After you left to get dressed, I told Tessa that." His smile was self-deprecating. "She didn't disagree."

"I see," Kristina murmured. Was that how these things were done among the upper crust, so cold-bloodedly? "It sounds as though you fired her the same as you did those executives in your company."

James shrugged. If he found the notion offensive, he didn't show it. "As I said, it was just business."

"Is that why you . . . ?" Kristina broke off. There were times when her mind got a head of her mouth. This was one of them.

"I what?" James asked.

"Nothing. Look, there's the castle."

Innishffarin lay directly ahead of them, shimmering in moonlight. The four corner towers stood etched against the sky, solid and indomitable, just as they had stood through all the centuries of turmoil and upheaval. For almost all that time, the proud castle had been under the guiding hand of men like the one at her side. Men who combined strength and honor as few had ever managed to do.

In the months she had spent sifting through the Wyndhams's past, she felt as though she had come to know them well. Not for a moment did she doubt that James was cut from the same cloth. Yet he was also undeniably different.

Even if he—as she was beginning to suspect—didn't realize it.

Different or not, he had one undeniably Wyndham characteristic—he didn't let anything drop. As he turned the Range Rover toward the car park on the far side of the draw bridge, he asked again, "I what?"

Kristina sighed. It was her own fault. Someday she was going to learn when to keep her mouth shut. Too bad it wouldn't come in time to help her with the present situation.

"Why you don't seem to mind about Tessa and Richard," she said reluctantly.

It was James's turn to look surprised, which was at least a little gratifying. "You have been busy," he said. "How long have you known about that?"

She sagged slightly, glad to have it confirmed that he really had known. "There was some talk in the village." That was true so far as it went but she wasn't about to tell him what she had overheard between his brother and his former fiancée.

There was no reason to, anyway. He undoubtedly already knew that they were afraid of him. He might even be enjoying it.

She turned slightly in the car seat and looked at him. He seemed completely relaxed but the impression was deceptive. His large, powerful hands clenched the steering wheel tightly enough for the knuckles to show white.

So he did care, but not about Tessa. Kristina didn't believe he was deceptive enough to pretend otherwise. There was something else. What had Richard said...that James believed he might have been involved in arranging the kidnapping?

A cold shiver ran down her back. At the time, the statement had passed unchallenged by her or anyone else, including James. Certainly he had not denied it.

Besides the enormity of such a crime, betrayal over a woman would be inconsequential. The outcome would rival the long-ago clash between Sir Reginald and his brother, which neither of them had survived.

She had never believed in the notion of the past repeating itself. As a historian, she knew that only the broadest and most general patterns might continue from one generation to the next. There was no reason to think that what had taken place within the walls of Innishffarin castle more than eight hundred years before could ever happen again.

No reason at all.

"You're cold," James said as he noticed her discomfort. He stripped off his evening jacket and draped it around her shoulders. The warmth and scent of him enveloped her. She closed her eyes for a moment and opened them to find him looking at her.

"Kristina McGinnis," he said gruffly, "you're not supposed to happen to me."

Her eyes widened, luminous with flecks of gold against the night. "I don't..." Understand she finished to herself, but she did, only too well. For he wasn't supposed to happen either, not here and now in her well-ordered life when everything was going along just as she wanted.

Not this complicated, oddly vulnerable man who made her forget all about prudence and good sense. Who made her feel so strangely, one with the ancient stones and soaring towers, the clash of the sea and over it all, moonlight pouring like molten silver.

Heat, too, was pouring through her veins as he drew her to him, gently but firmly. A soft gasp escaped her as he moved away from the steering wheel and lifted her over the gearshift in a single, effortless motion and settled her astride his lap.

The position was shockingly, deliciously intimate. The skirt of her tunic dress rode up, exposing her long, slender legs clear to the thighs.

He laughed deep in his throat and twined his fingers through her hair. Pale gold gleamed in his hands.

"Like sunlight," he murmured. "A woman with sunlight in her hair." Gently, he urged her head back, exposing the slender line of her neck. She felt his breath hotly caressing against her skin.

"I used to like the dark," he said, almost to himself. "Now..." His brows drew together as painful memory surged. "Sunlight," he said again, shaking off whatever images tormented him. His hand clasped the back of her head, holding her still, as his mouth raked down her throat.

Kristina cried out softly, her fingers digging into his broad shoulders. This was madness. She barely knew this man, he was still a stranger to her in so many vital ways. She had always been so reserved, restrained, even—truth be told—a little prudish. Her work was her life, it gave her purpose, satisfied her emotionally, kept her from ever feeling lonely or in need.

Or so she had always let herself believe. But now—sweet heaven, now!—everything had changed.

This was not herself, safe, sane, prudent Kristina McGinnis. Not this woman whose bare legs gleamed in the moonlight as she sat astride a powerful, hungry male, vividly aware of his arousal and, undeniably, her own.

Lightly, even delicately, the tip of his tongue traced the pulse beating beneath the almost translucent skin. He tasted her, savoring every inch, before he came at last to her mouth, full and parted, soft beneath the sudden devouring crush of his own.

He released her head but only to slide his hands down her back to her buttocks. Lifting her slightly, he palmed her bottom, moving her so that she was even more vividly conscious of his arousal.

Heat flared through her. She cried out softly far in the back of her throat. He caught the sound as his tongue thrust deeply. Her arms twined around his neck, her breasts, unbound beneath the tunic, rubbing against his chest. James groaned. He slipped his hands up under the loose fabric, grasping her narrow waist, reaching higher until he cupped her full, up-turned breasts.

The tunic concealed a great deal but not so the dress she had worn earlier. In his mind's eye, he saw her in it again, silver and white against the moon. Here in the shadows she was the same but different, all sunlight and honeyed warmth, her skin fragrant like heather crushed beneath his fingers and her body...full, ripe, wanting him.

His thumbs, callused from the years of rigorous exercise that had helped to keep him sane, raked lightly over her straining nipples. He circled the areolae gently, not yet touching the swollen tips, letting the passion within her build and build and...

A light slashed through the darkness. Kristina stiffened even as James let out a low curse. Near the entrance to the castle, a shadow appeared.

"Someone there?" a voice called.

"That's Ben," Kristina murmured. Her voice was breathless. It sounded as weak as she felt. "One of the students. He must have heard something."

James cursed again. He could feel her pulling away from him, quickly rearranging her clothing, not looking in his direction.

As she opened the door to get out, he put his hand over hers. "Come riding with me tomorrow." He knew a spot by a secluded pool, perfect for a picnic and whatever else might follow.

With her head still averted, she made a small gesture of refusal. "I can't. There's too much work to do. Besides..." She took a deep breath and turned to face him. Her eyes were dark, storm-tossed, filled with questions he could not answer.

"I don't want this to happen," she said quietly. "I'm just not prepared to deal with it."

His mouth twisted slightly. As recently as a few minutes before, he would not have believed the pain that cut through him at her words. Instinctively, he slammed down on it, denying that it existed, as he had learned—so painfully—to do.

"This what?" he asked, almost casually as though it really didn't matter.

She refused to join him in the pretense. "This between us. Whatever you want to call it, it's very powerful. I have a job to do, commitments to keep, and you have more than a few problems of your own to deal with. I just think..."

She broke off for a moment, faltering. Courage flowed with another breath but so, too, did sorrow. Wishing for the world to be different was surely the greatest folly but there were times when it couldn't be helped.

"I think we should keep our distance," she said finally.

Before he could answer, she got out of the Range Rover and walked quickly toward the castle.

James watched as she disappeared inside. He sat, silent and immovable in the darkness, his eyes gleaming silver. She was right, of course, in every way that ought to matter. Odd that none of them did.

The torrent raging in his blood cooled enough for him to relax slightly. He looked at the castle, proud and indomitable against the darkness, and knew a surge of possessiveness so powerful that it momentarily robbed him of breath. Innishffarin, heart and soul of his clan. His now and forever.

He thought of the woman who would soon be laying her head down to sleep within the thick walls of his stronghold, and smiled. She seemed to find nothing odd in fleeing from him, and from the emotions suddenly unleashed between them, to the very place that was his alone.

So be it. If he had learned anything in the past four years, he had learned patience. Indeed, he could fairly say that he had become a master at it. Besides, she was right, there were other issues that needed to be settled.

He gunned the motor and turned back onto the road to the manor. Behind him, the castle slumbered in the darkness. Only Kristina remained awake, staring at the stone ceiling above her pallet. She had traced the crude blocks a hundred times with her eyes before she realized she was not seeing them. He filled her mind as surely as he would have filled her body had she not fled when she did.

Madness, plain and simple. Moon-sent, heather-scent, faerie-addled madness. She would sleep it away, awakening to morning and the sweet reason of new day.

But first she dreamed—hot, quicksilver dreams—that mocked both reason and resolve, and left her, when morning did come at last, more uncertain even than before.

Chapter 6

Pride drove Kristina to rise early, wash all traces of the restless night from her face, and greet her students with a cheerful smile. She distributed the previous day's purchases and along with them made the announcement she had decided on in the wee hours of the morning.

"We've been working very hard and we've made great progress, so I think it's time for a break. I hereby declare a general amnesty from all work and endeavor saving those tasks necessary to the well-being of our animals and ourselves. In other words, go enjoy yourselves."

The whoops of astonished delight told her she was on the mark. Her students were as dedicated a bunch as could be found anywhere but they were also human. They needed time off just like everyone else.

As she watched them race off in all directions, chattering about what they were going to do with the

unexpected holiday, she breathed a small sigh of relief. She was doing what was right for them while also
giving herself some time alone to put her emotions in
order. That promised to be no easy task. To help her
with it, she decided to use the free hours for her personal project, searching for the Wyndham treasure.

She stopped first in the stone chapel and stood,
hands clasped before her, studying the magnificent
Wyndham Cross. It was an extraordinary work of
Byzantine craftsmanship, glittering with gold and
precious gems that managed to transcend the worldly
while still being extremely valuable in their own right.
One aspect of the modern world had been left untouched during the castle's restoration, namely the
sophisticated security system that protected the cross.
It had been installed a decade before and updated
several times, sad testimony to the fact that not even
the sacred was off-limits to thieves.

If Linus was right, the cross was a key part—but
only a part—of the treasure that the long-ago Wyndham had brought home from the Crusade. The problem was that no one else seemed to agree with her.
Richard had pooh-poohed the idea when she asked
him straight out. Everything there was to be found had
been. He had that on absolute authority, although he
wouldn't explain what that meant. Indeed, when she'd
tried to press him, he turned uncharacteristically reti-
cent and refused to say anything more on the subject.

No doubt about it, when it came to do with anything involving the Wyndham treasure, the family was
virtually mute. They'd never even revealed exactly
where the cross had been found or under what circumstances, only that it had been recovered "within
the grounds." That could mean anything from the

castle to the stables to the old pig mire. She shuddered at the thought. Perhaps she should just take the hint and give up but somehow she couldn't manage it. Careful, nit-picking, always-complaining Linus had her convinced there was far more still to be found. But where?

In the months since her arrival at the castle, she'd had little opportunity to really search. Now she resolved to do better. Within an hour of her announcement, the castle was deserted. Some of her students decided to walk into the village, others took a picnic down to the rocky beach. She was invited to go along on both excursions but begged off, saying that she had a few odds and ends to take care of.

After a final glance at Linus's journal—the book itself was too heavy and too fragile to carry around—she set off. In her hand was a map showing what was supposed to be every room in the castle. She had drawn it herself with painstaking care but the plain fact was that she didn't put much store in it. Any castle worth the name had at least a few hidden chambers and passages. Some of them would have been deliberately constructed while others would have occurred over the centuries as changes were made to the interior. Finding any of them would be difficult but she was determined to try.

By midday her determination—though still strong—was definitely dented. She was footsore, tired, and nursing a bruised left hand courtesy of an ill-advised attempt to move what had seemed to be a loose flagstone in the back passage between the seaward towers. For some unknown reason, that part of the castle kept drawing her.

Refusing to admit defeat, and with the afternoon still before her, she paused for a quick lunch. She was sitting out on the high sweep of the cliff overlooking the water, her knees drawn up to her chin and the remains of a sandwich beside her, when she realized she was no longer alone.

She knew, before she turned her head, who she would see. Moreover, she could not deny a sudden spurt of pleasure. James sat, silhouetted against the sky, on the dappled gray stallion. Behind him, fluffy white clouds moved across blue so bright it almost hurt the eyes. Gulls whirled overhead. The air was fragrant with the scents of spring. Unmoving, she watched as the stallion came slowly but steadily closer.

James frowned. He had not thought to find her alone. Indeed, he had counted on the presence of her students to make her less skittish of him. Instead, the castle was deserted save for the beautiful woman sitting pink-cheeked and wind-blown amid the heather.

He shook his head sardonically. He'd done his share of fantasizing while trapped in the dark of that Beirut hellhole, never knowing which day would be his last. But his imagination hadn't managed to come up with anything as provocative as Kristina McGinnis. She was completely outside his experience—real or imagined. He'd slept little and poorly last night. A dozen times he'd resolved to stay away from her for a while. God knew, he had enough to keep him busy.

But with morning, all his good intentions had gone flying out the window. He'd spent a few hours on the phone to London and then decided he needed a ride. The gray horse was obliging. With his master's hands light on the reins, he instinctively headed for Innish-ffarin.

James dismounted before he could let himself think of all the reasons why he shouldn't. He let the stallion graze and walked over to where Kristina was sitting. She had turned her head again and was looking out at the sea. Only the flush staining her cheeks revealed her emotions.

"Nice day," he said as he sat down beside her.

She murmured what he took to be agreement. They sat in silence for several minutes until she said softly, "I'm sorry."

James stiffened. "What for?"

Her answer was muffled but still understandable. "Letting things get out of hand."

He frowned. For reasons he didn't quite understand, her answer bothered him.

"It wasn't all your doing," he pointed out.

The words were mild enough but Kristina wasn't fooled. That was the sound of the male ego clanking. Hastily, she said, "No, of course not, I didn't mean that. But I do feel some responsibility."

"You tend to do that," he pointed out.

She looked at him curiously. "I do?"

He nodded. "You took responsibility for what you thought Tessa was feeling. You mother hen your students." He raised a hand in the direction of the castle. "You've even taken charge of a great, lumbering castle and made it shine like it hasn't in years." He tilted his head back, eyes closed, savoring the sunlight. Without looking at her, he added, "My guess is you're an eldest child, that or an only one."

"What makes you so sure?"

"I know the symptoms—takes responsibility including sometimes a disproportionate share of blame, has a talent for leadership but tends to shut off or deny conflicting urges, puts the welfare of others first but also tends to presume to know what's best. Sound familiar?''

"Embarrassingly. You do realize you're also describing yourself?"

"It takes one to know one."

"So you're saying we're cut from the same cloth?"

Light gleamed from beneath the slits of his eyes. His mouth lifted at the corners. "I'm not saying that at all. We're different in some very important and, I might say, very enjoyable ways."

He watched the color seep over her cheeks and laughed. More gently, he said, "Look, I know you were upset last night and I really don't want you to be. How about we start over?"

Kristina looked at him skeptically. Who was this man in well-worn riding clothes stretched out at her side as though he didn't have a care in the world? Surely not a man who had spent four years in hell and returned to find betrayal? He seemed impervious to the past, as though it did not exist.

But it did and the thought of all he was denying chilled her. Yet his offer was so tantalizing. Like it or not, understand it or not, she was deeply attracted to him.

Besides, she was only willing to run so far.

"Friends?" she asked tentatively.

"Most definitely," he said and held out his hand. His touch was warm and strong, yet reassuring in its restraint. She took it without thinking and allowed herself to be helped up.

"I've declared a holiday," she said by way of explanation as they walked back in the direction of the deserted castle. "The students needed little convincing to hotfoot it."

"Does that include yourself?"

She hesitated, thinking of Linus and the treasure. She had meant to spend the afternoon continuing her search but her hand still ached and the sunlit day danced before her eyes, tempting her unbearably. Last night, she had feared herself as much as him and had fled. But this was different, wasn't it? Bright, clear, safe.

"I suppose it does."

"Come for a ride. There's something I'd like to show you."

She looked down at the loose tunic she wore. "I'm not dressed for it. Besides, there are no extra horses here."

"There are at the manor and we've always kept riding clothes on hand for guests." When she still hesitated, he added, "Besides, you'll never find it on your own."

"Find what?"

"The Viking chapel," he said blandly and watched with amusement as she reacted.

"The *what?*"

"Not a very accurate name for it, I admit, but that's what it's been called for as long as anyone can remember. It's down the beach a few miles."

"In which direction?"

"That's for me to know."

Kristina hesitated. She knew perfectly well what he was doing. He wanted her company and he wasn't being overly scrupulous about how he got it. Ruefully, she thought that with another woman he might have dangled jewels or furs. She was offered an ancient ruin with an intriguing, if no doubt misleading, name. Whatever else might be said about him, James Wyndham was perceptive.

"All right," she said slowly, "I'll come. I'm certainly not accomplishing anything here."

"You're not supposed to on a holiday," he reminded her just before he whistled for the gray stallion. The big horse came at a gallop and stood patiently while James mounted.

"I'll get the Jeep," Kristina said hastily before he could suggest she join him. As this seemed to be a day for breaking rules, hauling out the one and only vehicle at the castle caused hardly a twinge. It hadn't been used in months and she breathed a sigh of relief when it started on the first try.

The vehicle was advertised as off-road but she'd never trusted it that far. James called out that he'd meet her at the manor. He took the more direct route across the rolling green fields and was waiting for her when she got there.

Half an hour later, with Kristina suitably clad in a white linen shirt, tan jodhpurs and a tweed jacket, they rode out. Her mount was a spirited chestnut mare who kept her fully occupied for the first few minutes. James watched out of the corner of his eye but said nothing. When at last Kristina won the contest and the mare settled down, he laughed.

"You're persistent."

She tossed her head, looked in his direction and said, "I'm lots of things. Come on, I'll race you."

Before he could reply, she was off. The mare needed only the gentlest urging. She knew the terrain well and surged over it joyfully. A dirt path led from the cliff side down to the beach. Sunlight sparkled over the water. White-flecked waves played catch with tiny sandpipers that raced in and out along the surf. Gulls circled overhead and far out along the rocky promontory, sleeping seals glinted darkly.

Kristina pulled up as James joined her. For a time, they rode in silence along the sandy shore. The beach widened beyond the castle. Dunes dotted with sea grass rolled lazily inland. The cliffs changed to small rises and eventually gave way entirely near the point where a river emptied into the sea.

"This way," James said and pointed toward a rough outcropping of rocks near the river's edge. They dismounted there and left the horses to graze. Slowly, Kristina studied what had been a simple enclosure.

"Older than Innishffarin," she said, almost to herself.

James nodded. "By several centuries at least. The original keep at Innishffarin was built of dressed stones and stood about fifty feet high. That's a whole lot more sophisticated than this ever was."

He ran a hand over one of the rough stones mottled with lichen. They appeared to have been piled up just as they were taken from the surrounding earth, perhaps in haste when shelter was needed from the elements.

"Why is it called the Viking chapel?" Kristina asked as she bent down and brushed dirt away from the base of the stones. As she had suspected, the building extended underground.

"It's presumed to have been built by Vikings and I suppose the shape reminded people of some of the early chapels around here."

"I've seen something like this before on Orkney, a place called Skara Brae. But that's far older than the Vikings. Has there ever been an excavation?"

James shook his head. His gaze was focused on the supple line of her back as she bent to her task. Her pale hair spilled over her shoulders, veiling her face. He moved closer and caught the faint, elusive scent of her—heather and sunshine, lavender and woman. He took a deep breath, struggling for the control that had always come to him so readily and yet which now was so painfully elusive.

He had not changed, on that he was determined. Beirut was over, past, done with. It had no more importance than a particularly unpleasant nightmare. Exactly as he had expected himself to do, he had picked up the threads of his life right where he had left them. Granted a few changes had been necessary, Tessa among them. But nothing of any significance had been altered, certainly not himself. The terrorists had beaten him, chained him, tormented him, and robbed him of four years of his life. But they had not changed him. He would never give them that.

He had returned to his life as strong and resolute as he had always been. Emotional vulnerabililty was for other men; men like Richard who had never had to carry the responsibility for a family, a business, a history. Richard could afford to follow his lusts wherever they happened to lead him. But for James, the only safety lay in control.

Control that Kristina McGinnis severely threatened.

He had been a fool to come after her. Only the memory of the pain in her eyes the night before had driven him to want to reassure and comfort her. Ruefully, he acknowledged that he seemed to have succeeded in doing that. She was completely relaxed and at ease with him. It was his turn to be uncertain.

Enough of that. The day was perfect, the company was good and he was free. He really would be a fool if he thought about anything else.

"Hungry?" he asked as Kristina stood and brushed her hands off.

Surprised, she nodded. "As a matter of fact, I am. It must be the sea air. Too bad we didn't think to bring anything with us."

"Who didn't? No sensible Scotsman goes anywhere without the basics." He laughed at her doubtful look and pointed to the saddlebag he had taken off the gray horse. "Take a look in there while I round up some fire wood."

When he returned a few minutes later with an armload of logs and kindling, Kristina was sitting cross-legged on the ground studying what she had found.

"Matches, plates, forks and knives, crystal wine-glasses, white wine, and a container of very nice strawberries. Is it possible you forgot something?"

"Sounds like it. Weren't there any napkins?"

"As a matter of fact there were along with a small tablecloth. Oh, yes, there was also this." She held up a length of sturdy, finely woven netting. "However, it doesn't look edible."

"Have faith," James said. He scooped out a slight depression in the ground, encircled it with small stones, and set the kindling inside. The small twigs and branches caught quickly. When the fire was going, he fed in several smaller logs and waited until they were also burning well. Satisfied, he got up and reached for the netting.

"I'll be back in a few minutes. There's a rock pool over there. You can put the wine in to chill." With the net in hand, he disappeared over the ridge behind the enclosure.

Kristina watched him go before she got to her feet. The pool was only a short distance away, hidden by the rocky ledge that surrounded it. Part of the ledge seemed to be man-made and to have been constructed the same way as the enclosure. She was musing over who might have done it as she lowered the wine bottle into the chill depths. A bit of the water splashed against her lips as she removed her hand. To her surprise, she discovered that it was fresh. Even this close to the shore, the salt sea had not tainted it. She took a long drink and splashed more on her face. For a few minutes, she was content to enjoy the sunshine and fragrant air. But before long curiosity got the better of her. She rose and walked slowly in the direction James had gone.

She found him crouched beside a rushing stream that fed the pool. He had removed his jacket and shirt. Sunlight poured over his bare shoulders and back. With a start, she realized that he must have been spending as much time as possible in the sun.

Her stomach tightened. She walked closer on silent feet until she was standing directly behind him. He turned his head slightly but said nothing. Below where he crouched, she glimpsed the net stretched underwater. The surface of the water sparkled but below were deep shadows, irregularities in the stream bed, rocks, and . . .

Something moved, thrusting quicksilver in the flow. The net blossomed, straining to its limits, caught on the rocks to which it had been anchored, and held.

James stood in a single, smooth motion, grabbed both ends of the net, pulled them together, and tossed his catch onto the bank. The salmon flopped briefly and was still.

Kristina gasped. She had never seen so powerful and elusive a fish caught so stealthily. "How did you...?"

He laughed, pleased with her surprise. "Never gone seining, have you?"

She shook her head. "I've seen it in old illustrations but I've never known anyone to do it."

"A rod and a line are easier. Seining calls for more patience and more luck."

"It seems you have both," Kristina said softly.

He rose, the fish in his hand. "Aye, it seems I do."

She followed him back to the stone enclosure and the fire. When he drew a dirk from his boot and began to clean the fish, Kristina stopped him. "I'll do that," she said.

He glanced at her for a moment before nodding. "I'll get the wine."

She worked quickly. When she was done, she wove a lattice of green wood twigs, slipped the fish inside and set it to cook.

James returned with the wine. He had put his shirt back on but left it unbuttoned. The riding jacket hung from a low branch where Kristina had also put hers. The day was growing warmer.

She turned the fish, placed it back on the fire and accepted a glass of the wine he had opened. It was crisp and cool on her tongue. High above, a hawk turned lazily.

"I used to come seining when I was a boy," James said quietly. He twirled the crystal wineglass between his fingers, watching as it caught the light. "I'd stay out for days, camping under the stars, eating whatever I could forage. There were times when I imagined I could go on like that forever.''

''What changed your mind?''

''Rain usually. A good, icy downpour can bring even a thirteen-year-old to his senses.''

Kristina laughed. She had her own memories of days spent free in the wilderness, civilization left safely behind. Nothing would ever replace the sheer golden joy of them.

''Did Richard come with you?''

His mouth thinned. ''Sometimes.'' He glanced toward the fire. ''The fish is done.''

She took the hint. They ate in silence and greedily for the salmon deserved their full attention. When it was gone and the wineglasses refilled, Kristina lay back against the fragrant grass, her eyes half closed, and gazed up at the sky. The hawk was gone, perhaps having hunted successfully.

The utter peacefulness of the day, her full stomach and an unaccustomed indulgence in wine at midday combined to make Kristina's eyes grow heavy. Sleep stole over her.

She woke a short time later disoriented. Several moments passed before she realized where she was and that she was alone. James's riding jacket still hung from the tree but there was no sign of him. For that matter, the plates were also gone although the small linen tablecloth remained spread out on the grass.

She stood and looked around uncertainly. The horses grazed a short distance away. In the afternoon stillness, she heard the water.

He was in the pool, cutting through it with sure, swift strokes. His head was down, his head turned only slightly to the side. Beneath the dappled surface, his big, lithe body shone darkly.

On the bank, arranged neatly, were the plates. He had washed them.

Kristina took a step forward. She had no intention of joining him in the water. The brief interlude in front of the castle the night before had taught her that this was a man she had to handle as cautiously as fire. But neither would she retreat. She was, she told herself sternly, no naive schoolgirl, presuming there still were such things.

He surfaced just then and stood, waist-deep in the water. His hands were on his hips as he flung his head back, showering droplets in all directions. He looked startled to see her.

"You looked out of it. I thought you'd sleep longer."

"I guess not. How's the water?"

"Good." He hesitated and to her amusement, his cheeks darkened. "Look, I really wasn't expecting company."

Kristina's gaze fell on his trousers which were hanging from a hawthorn bush, waving like a pennant in the breeze.

"Guess not," Kristina said mildly. She liked him suddenly, so much in fact that it went like a shock through her. Desire she had already felt, curiosity and compassion as well. But this simple affection for a man who could seem so self-assured and worldly and yet still be embarrassed at being found starkers—as the British said—quite won her heart. It made her feel as though she had been given a trust that she could not abuse.

"I'll just check on the horses," she said and withdrew.

He joined her a few minutes later. His hair was damp and he looked as though he had dressed hastily but he was also smiling.

"You ought to try it," he said. "I'd forgotten how good it feels."

"Another time. I should be getting back."

"I thought this was a holiday."

"It is," she admitted, "for the students, but there are always things I need to be doing. Paperwork, if nothing else. The nice people who approved my grants like to be kept up-to-date on our progress."

"Hang progress, it's overrated. Besides, if you're authentic, how do you manage it? No phone, no typewriter, certainly no computer. You must resort to vellum and a quill."

"I bend the rules," she said absently. The mention of vellum reminded her of Linus. She was about to mention the illuminated manuscript when she stopped. She hadn't minded Richard thinking her a little foolish for bringing up the Wyndham Treasure; his opinion simply didn't count all that much. But James's did. She cared very much what he thought.

Still, there'd be no harm in seeing what she might be able to learn, provided she was discreet.

"Speaking of the rules," she said, "there's something I've been wondering about. As part of my contract, I'm supposed to be preparing as complete a history of the castle as I can manage. A great deal of it's already done but there are some omissions. The Wyndham Cross, for instance. I've read the story about its discovery that's in all the guidebooks but I haven't found any mention of where exactly it was found or how. Would you happen to know?''

James didn't answer at once. He walked over to the fire and began covering it with sand. When he was satisfied the flames were out, he stood slowly, brushed his hands clean and gave her a long, level look.

''It was found in the early 1800s by Angus and Katlin Wyndham, my forebearers. They weren't actually married at the time but they were wed a short while later. Katlin Wyndham was a Sinclair by birth. The less said about that, probably the better. They found the cross, restored the castle, and lived a long, happy life together. What more do you need to know?''

''Where exactly was it found?'' Kristina asked. He'd given her the standard day-tripper version, except the passing mention of the animosity between the Wyndhams and the Sinclairs. She wanted more.

Still, James hesitated. ''Oddly enough, we've never discussed it much.''

''Why not?''

''I'm not sure. Force of habit, perhaps. The Wyndhams have always tended to be closemouthed about their affairs. Considering some of the things we've gotten up to, it was just as well.''

''Never mind the rest of it, it's the cross I want to know about. Was it actually found at the castle?''

''Of course it was,'' James said, looking puzzled. ''Where else could it have been?''

''I don't know. Since you won't say, there's been all sorts of speculation. That Angus Wyndham actually found it in Constantinople, for instance, got it in some sort of illegal transaction and concocted the story about finding it at Innishffarin to defuse a nasty diplomatic situation.''

"That's ridiculous," James said. He looked genuinely angry. "They found it in the sea cave. Katlin Sinclair could have died in the process of finding it. It was only luck that Angus realized where she'd gone. They redid the chapel in gratitude and baptized every one of their six children there. Constantinople be damned."

"Okay, okay," Kristina said hastily, "so it was legit. What's this about a sea cave?" Her ears were prickling. For the first time she knew what that meant; it felt itchy.

"It's in the side of the cliff near Innishffarin," James said reluctantly. "Or at least it was. Who knows if it still exists. The entrance was walled over not long after the cross was found, the passage being too dangerous. Nobody's set foot in it since the day almost two hundred years ago when Angus and Katlin removed the cross."

Kristina's face fell. Walled over? Sweet heaven, she'd probably have no chance of finding it if that were the case.

"Are you sure?" she asked.

"Absolutely. Angus kept detailed records about everything to do with the Wyndham properties, including the castle. As I recall, he spent two pounds, nine shillings on a top-notch mason to make sure the job would be done right. I've seen it noted down in one of his account books."

"Sounds as though he was a good businessman," Kristina said grudgingly.

"It runs in the family. Anything else you'd like to know?"

Yes, most definitely. She wanted to know if there was another entrance but she couldn't bring herself to ask. If she did, she'd have to explain about Linus and her belief that most of the treasure had yet to be found, with all the amusement that would no doubt provoke. The damn, superior Wyndhams thought they knew everything about their history and they were mostly right. But she was still convinced there was something they'd missed.

Casting around for any lead that might be useful, however faint, she asked, "How did Angus and Katlin manage to locate the sea cave?"

"It's a long story," James said, "and not especially interesting. Did you happen to see which way the horses have gone?"

"They're off grazing somewhere. I like long stories. There's no hint in the guidebooks. What exactly tipped them off?"

James sighed. It was a purely male sound and as such, long suffering. "It has to do with the ghost," he said finally.

Kristina's eyes widened. "The what?"

"You heard me, lass. The Wyndham ghost. Innishffarin was haunted for a time by the shade of the laird who lost the place to the Sinclairs. He vowed to stay put until the treasure was found. Once it was—and the castle regained through marriage—he departed, or so the tale goes. At any rate, nothing's been seen of him since, presuming there ever was to start with."

"How come your family has kept this to themselves all these years?"

"Because it's daft, that's why. Don't tell me you believe in ghosts?"

"I don't know if I do or not," Kristina admitted. Her mind was working overtime. Was that why Richard—and seemingly all the Wyndhams—believed no treasure remained? Because the *ghost* was no longer in evidence? Well, sure, why not? It was as good a reason as any.

"Historians usually like to rely on something a little more substantial," she said as mildly as she could manage.

James shrugged. "It was all over and done with a long time ago."

So far as he was concerned, that was the end of the matter. She finished cleaning up while he saddled the horses. When they were ready, James helped her to mount. His hand rested warm on her calf as he looked at her perched on the chestnut horse's back. She went very still, acutely aware of his touch and trying desperately not to let him see it. He had kept his word, the outing had been purely friendly. It wasn't his fault that she was so susceptible to him, even to the extent of feeling a small twist of regret at how easily he seemed to forget what had passed between them the previous evening.

It was better this way by far. They would go their separate ways, maintaining a cordial friendship in the process, but with none of the explosive sensuality that so threatened the steady calmness of her world. Far better, if not half so interesting.

Having come to this conclusion in her own mind, Kristina was not at all prepared when James looked up at her and with no warning, asked, "Would you like to come to London with me?"

Chapter 7

"London?" Kristina repeated. Even to her own ears, she sounded breathless, as though the wind had been knocked from her. Which, in a sense, it had.

"You know," James said as he swung into the saddle, "that big city south of here. Nice theaters, one or two decent restaurants, a river down the middle. London."

"I don't think..."

"You have to go there anyway, to report to the government gurus who funded part of your grant. It's a requirement of getting the money, isn't it?"

"How did you know that?"

"I read the file. You sent all the details to Richard when you applied for permission to use the castle. It's all there, including the fact that you have to report in."

"That was left fairly open," Kristina said.

"But there's no sense putting it off. After all, these are tight fiscal times. Best to get in there while you can and remind them of what a sterling job you're do-ing."

"Still, I don't think . . ."

"There's no reason why we shouldn't keep each other company, is there?"

Kristina opened her mouth and shut it again. There was no way she could explain why turning down his invitation made sense, at least not without sounding like a cross between an overheated adolescent and a maiden school marm with a too-tight bun. Drat.

"Now that you mention it," she said calmly, "it sounds perfect."

As perfect as taking a running jump off a roof but there was no sense going into that now. It was suffi-cient that he looked momentarily surprised by her ready agreement. Only momentarily, mind. He recov-ered with his usual aplomb.

"Tomorrow?" he asked.

Tomorrow she'd been hoping to get a few hours to herself to begin searching for the sea cave, but it would have to wait.

"Tomorrow," she confirmed and spurred the chestnut horse on.

"Now don't worry about a thing," Frank Standish said. "We'll take care of everything here and you're going to do fine. Heck, they'll probably try to give you *more* money."

Kristina sighed. It had come to this. Her own stu-dents having to comfort and reassure her because she was in such a stew—they thought—about going be-fore the grant board. Ever since she'd told them the previous evening that she would be spending a few days in London discussing the project, they'd been falling all over themselves to be nice to her.

She appreciated it but the guilt was a little hard to deal with. Those butterflies that had taken up residence in her stomach had nothing at all to do with the grant. They had James Wyndham written on them, every last one.

She shook her head. Writing on butterflies? Gruesome thought. Get a grip, girl, she murmured to herself and for good measure rammed the felt cloche down more snugly on her head. It was raining again, never mind that it was spring. The rain held more than a tinge of ice.

Her raincoat was belted snugly around her waist, she had put on her sensible boots and she had a selection of equally sensible clothes packed away in her bag. Sensible Kristina McGinnis was on her way to London—with a man she barely knew who somehow made her forget all her sane, sensible self.

They were flying out of Edinburgh. James had arranged to pick her up a nine a.m. On the dot, he pulled up and got out of the car to help her. Frank eyed him warily. Kristina couldn't blame the younger man. In old riding clothes, the laird of Innishffarin was impressive. In a dark worsted Saville Row suit, armored as it were in authority and success, he was formidable.

"All set?" he asked as he opened the hatch and deposited her bag. Next to it was a hand-tooled leather suitcase, old and venerable, that looked as though it had been around the world at least once and was the better for the experience.

"I guess," Kristina said. As set as she was ever going to be. She took a deep breath, gave Frank a smile she didn't feel and got into the Rover.

"What time is the flight?" she asked as they drove away from the castle.

"Whatever time we get there. Sure you've got everything you need?"

"How about a road map?" Kristina muttered.

James cast her a quick glance. "What did you say?"

"A map. I feel as though I'm in uncharted territory."

He laughed and eased up a little on the gas, enough so that he could turn and look at her for a moment. "The plane belongs to the firm," he said when his eyes were once again back on the road. "One of our subsidiaries makes them, so it would look a bit strange if we didn't fly it ourselves. Aside from the convenience of having it there when it's needed, it's considerably slower and more cramped than a commercial jet. Plus there's no movie."

"Forget it then. I'm not going."

"But it does beat the train."

"Oh, all right."

"You're a good sport."

"About the plane," she said, lest there be any misunderstanding. "Otherwise, I can be downright prickly."

"Really?" he inquired. "I hadn't noticed."

"The hell you didn't."

"Professor McGinnis, I'm shocked. What kind of language is that from a woman of scholarship and erudition?"

He didn't look shocked, Kristina thought grumpily. He looked pleased with himself, even just a tiny bit smug. Although it was hard to tell, really. He had that hooded look around the eyes again, the kind he got whenever he was thinking deep, as her mother used to say.

She settled back against the seat and let her own eyes close. Sometimes the smartest thing a woman could do was keep her own thoughts to herself.

The plane was just as he'd said, cramped. There were two seats on either side of a central aisle, room for ten in all plus a crew of two. The pilot was appropriately silver-haired and courteous, dressed in a navy blue uniform with a discreet patch on his shoulder that read Wyndham Industries. The copilot was the same only younger, black-haired instead of silver, but otherwise cut from the same mold.

The plane smelled of leather, good wool carpeting, artificially processed air and the scent of aviation fuel. It was an unmistakably masculine scent, redolent of powerful machinery lightly garbed in luxury.

As she settled into her seat and pulled the safety belt snug, Kristina said, "Tell me you don't fly this thing?"

"Why would I?" James asked, looking puzzled.

"Oh, I don't know. It seems like it ought to go with the job." She'd read her share of romance novels. High-powered tycoons with private planes always flew them.

"I've got a pilot for that," he said, sitting down beside her. "I don't know the first thing about flying. Well, no, that's not true. I do know how the plane stays up."

"How?" Kristina asked. She had taken off her raincoat, stowing it overhead, and pulled off the cloche. Her hair tumbled loose and slightly damp around her shoulders.

She was suddenly very conscious of him so close to her in the small confines of the cabin. He was a big man, tall and broad-shouldered, and he seemed to take up all the available space. In reality, he did no such thing but the impression was so strong that she couldn't shake it.

"Sheer force of will," he said.

Her eyes widened. "Oh, no, not you, too?"

"You're another one?"

She nodded jerkily. "I've never understood why seemingly intelligent people can get in these things and just trust that they'll *fly*. Do they see any feathers? Do they hear a single chirp? No, but in they get, never a second thought. Forget about gravity, universal laws, all that sort of thing. I'm in a hurry to get to Disney World or Timbuktu or wherever, so I'll just *fly*. Right."

James leaned back in his chair, unbuttoned his suit jacket, and smiled. "What a relief. I can fake it with the best of them, but the fact is I hate flying. Always have."

"Then why do it?"

"Because I hate it," he said, as though that ought to be obvious. "I don't like to fly because it scares me, so I have to do it."

"It wouldn't occur to you to take a bus?" Kristina asked.

"To where? New York, Los Angeles, Tokyo? I used to spend a good part of my life traveling between places that were thousands of miles apart. It was key to my business. If I couldn't do it, I couldn't achieve what I'd set out to do."

"Do you always face down your fears that way?"

"I try," he said shortly and reached into his inside pocket. "How about a little gin rummy?"

The engines revved. Quickly, Kristina nodded. "Penny a point?"

"Let's be wild. Loser buys dinner."

Kristina picked a seafood place a few blocks away from the company apartment James had insisted she use. He was, as he explained, staying elsewhere. She got to pick because he was paying.

She'd won by a couple of dozen points right toward the end as the plane was coming into Gatwick airport. The downward slant of the aircraft had surprised her. The flight had gone by more quickly than she would have thought possible.

A London taxi in all its glory met them on the tarmac. At least it looked like a taxi. In fact, it was privately owned, James's version of a Rolls-Royce. He pointed out that it got better mileage, had fewer breakdowns, and attracted less undesirable attention. It also had a great stereo system that played vintage Beatles all the way into the city.

The apartment was in one of the newer buildings set on a curve of the Thames river with a view of Tower Bridge. Someone with a fondness for chintz had been let loose in it. The results weren't bad, just overwhelming. Kristina dumped her bag in the oversize bedroom, told herself she still had both feet firmly planted on the ground and went off to dinner.

James met her in the lobby. They walked the short distance to the restaurant. The rain had stopped and the air was balmy. All the affection she felt for London came welling back as they dodged a motorbike, jumped over a puddle and pushed through the door of the restaurant.

It was crowded but a table was found. The waiter brought oversize menus, advised them that the crab wasn't bad and departed. The tables were covered with brown paper upon which sat canisters of paper napkins and bottles of hot sauce. Several people seated nearby had purple hair.

"Come here often?" James asked after a glance around. He loosened his tie, took a swallow of the beer they'd ordered right off, and eyed her benignly.

"Wait," she advised, "you're in for a treat. I studied in London for a year. This place practically kept me alive."

"Probably keeps a few cockroaches in the same state," he remarked good-naturedly. Before she could answer, the waiter returned. Leisurely service was not a hallmark of the establishment.

"So?" he inquired.

"Crab," Kristina said.

"Same," James added.

The waiter grunted and went off. Around them, the conversation swirled. People were laughing, talking, arguing. Kristina and James stared at each other. At length, he cleared his throat and asked, "How did a girl who grew up in a fishing camp end up a medieval historian?"

"Just lucky, I guess." She tossed back an oyster cracker and added, "I didn't want to marry the boy next door—actually he lived two miles downstream— and I had a peculiar love of old places. In the States, it was hard to find very many. So I came to England, went to school for a while, and the rest just happened."

"And the boy?"

Kristina laughed. "He went into the mail-order computer business, made a mint and retired to the Caribbean. Fact is, I blew it."

"You don't sound too upset."

"I like my work. What about you?"

"I like your work, too."

"No, I'm serious. Did you ever think of doing anything besides running Wyndham Industries?"

He considered that for a moment before he shook his head. "No, I never did. I was the eldest son. Richard wasn't interested. There was never any question what I would do."

"Yet Richard's been running the firm the last few years and he doesn't seem to have made too much of a mess of it."

He frowned and she feared she had gone too far mentioning his brother. The waiter arrived just then, bearing platters overladen with succulent pink crab and all the trimmings. He plopped them down on the table, took an order for a couple more beers and departed.

"He's done all right," James said finally. He cracked a crab claw, forked out the meat, and added, "Better than I thought he would, to be honest."

"You worried about it?"

"I worried about a lot of things, principally whether or not I'd live through the day. But the fate of the business was definitely on the list."

"So Richard's off the hook?"

"I wouldn't go that far. This isn't bad."

The food was delicious but she let that go. "I get the impression Richard cares a great deal about what you think of him."

"What makes you think that?"

"Just an idea I've got." The fact that his brother looked ready to jump out of his skin every time James got near him had something to do with it.

"Has it occurred to you that it might be a guilty conscience?" James asked.

"It has," she admitted reluctantly. "But I don't think it's about what you think it's about."

He took another bite of the crab. "What do I think it's about?"

"Lebanon, the kidnapping."

"And what is it about?"

"Tessa and the fact that it was you who went through hell and not him."

"You're sure about this?"

"No," she admitted, "of course not. It's just instinct."

He smiled. "Woman's intuition?"

"If you must. Do you honestly think your brother arranged for you to be kidnapped?"

"I honestly think we shouldn't discuss this," he said. More gently, he added, "It's bad for the digestion."

Kristina fell silent. She was surprised he'd tolerated her questions as long as he had. When they came right down to it, whatever had happened between the brothers was none of her business.

The crab dwindled, the crowd thinned and an hour or so later James walked her back to the apartment.

"So what did you think of it?" she asked. "Tell the truth."

"I had a better meal once," he said thoughtfully. "It was a little place in Ankara, did a thing with lamb and rice you wouldn't believe. But this was a close second."

She felt absurdly pleased that he'd approved her choice. They reached the building and were admitted by the doorman. Outside, the roar of traffic was constant but muted. The lobby was done in late yuppie, lots of marbleized wallpaper and art deco furnishings. On the top floor, where the elevator left them, silence reigned.

"Thank you for dinner," she said as James took the key from her and slipped it into the lock. He opened the door and stood aside for her to enter.

"You won fair and square," he said and kissed her. He gathered her up into his arms, drew her close against him, put a hand under her chin and tilted her head back. His mouth was warm and inviting. He tasted her lightly, coaxingly. When she moaned—for the pleasure sweeping through her was sweet indeed—he deepened the kiss.

His chest was hard and unyielding against her. Through the layers of clothing, she could feel the powerful muscles and sinew, the driving will, the unrelenting masculinity.

Under other circumstances, his aggressiveness might have frightened her. But with James she felt curiously safe, as though some hidden part of herself recognized that he would never hurt her.

Indeed, she feared her own impulses far more than she did his. It would be so very easy to take another step into the room, and another... To forget everything except her consuming need for this man.

His body was warm and hard against her own. The night stretched before them. So many hours... alone, in darkness, hidden. So tempting.

The elevator doors opened. James cursed under his breath and pressed her discreetly into the shadows of the entrance. Voices touched them—a man and a woman, laughing over something they had seen at the theater.

The moment was gone. They stood, a little awkwardly, and stared at one another.

James touched a white linen handkerchief to his mouth. Huskily, he said, "That answers one question."

"What?" Her voice sounded very far away and not at all like her own.

"The other night was no fluke."

"Is that what you thought?"

He looked at her for a long moment. "It's what I hoped."

His bluntness robbed her of breath. There was a twisting pain in her chest. She turned away only to be stopped by his hand on her arm.

"Life's complicated, Professor. I've got enough to deal with. I don't need to be spending every waking hour thinking about a woman with sun in her hair."

"Then don't," she said, fighting the pain. She should have known, should have seen this, should have protected herself better. Stupid, so stupid to let herself feel this much. He was wounded and wouldn't admit it, hurting badly and in full denial, and she was there, right smack in the middle of his path, only asking for trouble. Stupid.

"Go away," she said, and meant it.

He made a harsh sound deep in his throat and let go of her. "That's exactly what I had in mind."

Her legs felt weak. She leaned back against the wall, hardly knowing that she did so. He walked down the hall, stopped in front of the next apartment and took out a key.

"What are you doing?"

"Turning in. It's been a long day."

"I don't..."

"The firm owns the building," he said. His mouth thinned. "I use this apartment whenever I'm in London. We keep several others for guests."

At her look of surprise, his manner gentled slightly. "Get some sleep. You've got to face the grant board tomorrow."

The door shut behind him.

Chapter 8

The grant board was made up of eight pinstripe-suited gentlemen ranging in age from thirty-something to infinity, but all looking disconcertingly alike. They met in a chamber—it was too grand to be called a room—within the sound of Big Ben and the sight of Parliament. The walls were twenty feet high and paneled in teak. The ceiling was ornately molded. A selection of portraits—all of stern gentlemen in velvet and ermine—scrutinized the proceedings.

In the center of the room was a large table polished to a high sheen by generations of dutiful servants. The eight gentlemen sat on one side of the table. Kristina sat in a chair facing them.

"And so," she said, winding up, "the project remains within budget and slightly ahead of schedule. As you know, student enrollment was higher than anticipated indicating considerable interest in the experience of actually 'living' in the past. Innishffarin has provided a rare opportunity, one that I hope can be repeated in the future. The support of this board is greatly appreciated. Now if you have any questions, I will do my best to answer them.''

She waited, trying to guess what the august gentlemen might throw at her but they merely glanced at one another and nodded.

"Nicely done, Professor," the chairman said. "I think you've covered everything we could reasonably expect. Money is dreadfully tight this year but when is it not? I believe I speak for the rest when I say we are satisfied with your progress. Do keep in touch but in the meantime, you can rest assured that your funding will continue."

Kristina breathed a surreptitious sigh of relief. It had gone even better than she had hoped.

"Thank you," she said as she stood and began gathering up her papers. The gentlemen rose as well. It was time for lunch. They parted with mutual smiles and handshakes all around. Moments later, Kristina stood on the sidewalk, breathing what passed for fresh air and giving silent thanks that the interview was over. She had managed to get through it despite the fact that she'd had almost no sleep and was as distracted as she'd ever been in her life. No wonder she'd tended to steer clear of emotional entanglements in the past. They were hell on her peace of mind and not much good for her looks, either. Her eyes felt gritty, she had a headache, and the butterflies in her stomach seemed to be holding a Roller Derby. She'd skipped breakfast but the thought of food had no appeal. Neither did much of anything else. She was standing there, unsure of what to do next, when the problem solved itself.

"Got a light?" a voice asked.

She turned. Richard was lounging against the wall, dressed in a three-piece suit that would have gotten him into the stuffiest club in London but with tousled hair and a grin crooked enough to be endearing.

"You don't have a cigarette," she pointed out, not unreasonably.

He shrugged and came over to join her. "I quit a year ago. Trouble is I haven't learned any new pick up lines since then."

Despite herself, she laughed. "Is that what this is?"

"Not exactly," he admitted. "I thought we might have a drink, get a little better acquainted. I realized the other evening that I don't really know much about what you're doing at the castle. It does sound fascinating, though. How about filling me in?"

"All right," Kristina agreed. She was in no hurry to return to the apartment and besides, Richard interested her, if only because he was James's brother.

"How did you happen to show up here?" she asked as he took her arm. They headed across the street.

"A chap on the board called this morning to say you'd be coming by, wanted to know if I cared to sit in."

"And you didn't?"

"Not really. I'm keeping a rather low profile these days. Besides, what he really wanted to know was if I was still at the usual number."

"I don't follow."

"At Wyndham, at the firm, or if James had booted me out, as the betting has it he's about to do."

"I see," Kristina said slowly. "Do you think that's what he's planning?"

They dodged a double-deck bus and made it to the other side. "I've no idea," Richard said. "That's the problem. We used to be able to talk to each other but not anymore. He's shut me out completely. The worst part is that I can't even blame him for it. He's been through hell—he's entitled to a few resentments. But I can't live with it, either. Which is where you come in."

"I don't really see . . ."

"Are you hungry?" She shook her head.

"Drink?"

"No thanks. Look, Richard, I'd like to help but..."

"Let's walk then. Hear me out, that's all I'm asking. It's not easy my doing this, you know. I just don't know where else to turn."

Kristina fell silent. They kept walking until they entered the greensward of Saint James's Park off Whitehall. Richard, looking suddenly tired, found a bench within sight of the pelicans floating on the pond.

"Damn silly looking bird," he muttered. "All mouth, no brain."

"Very well adapted for survival," Kristina countered as she sat down beside him.

He laughed, loudly enough to startle some of the smaller species of birds roosting in the trees near the bench. "Might be right for them but that doesn't work too well with humans. Letting our appetites run away with us, I mean. Prescription for disaster, actually."

He ought to know, Kristina thought, but she didn't say so. It would have been cruel and besides, Richard didn't seem to need any prompting. He had made up his mind he was going to talk to her and nothing, not even her own disinclination, was going to stop him.

She wouldn't have been human if she hadn't felt curious about what he was going to say. But she was also uncomfortable. After all, he barely knew her. She had no real connection to the Wyndhams. Surely there was a family friend, a minister, someone who would be better suited?

Unless, of course, he was aware that she had come down to London with James and had jumped to certain conclusions about their relationship.

"You're not his usual type," Richard said suddenly. He was looking straight ahead but he shifted his glance slightly to see what reaction this would get.

It got none. Kristina knew better. She watched the pelicans and waited.

Richard sighed. He leaned back on the bench, stretched out his legs, and squinted at the sun. "Of course, neither was Tessa, but that was business."

Still nothing. He sat up straighter, clasped his hands between his knees and got serious. "I made a damn fool of myself over Tessa, but the fact is, I'm genuinely fond of her. I have reason to believe she feels the same way about me. We were thrown together under the most god-awful circumstances. I can't begin to tell you what it was like those first few days and weeks after James was kidnapped. The securities markets turned completely against us, some of our banks started talking about canceling lines of credit that had been in place for years, it could have been a debacle. Tessa stuck with me, convinced me I could hold things together. People think she's totally frivolous but she put in eighteen-hour days helping me. I wouldn't have made it without her. It wasn't until later—*much later*—that anything personal developed."

Kristina was tempted to ask if that had been when it began to look as though James might never be coming home, but she stopped herself. Whatever Tessa and Richard's motives might have been, they were none of her business.

"Besides," he went on, "James doesn't care anything about this. He wrote Tessa off without a second thought."

"I'd think you'd be glad of that under the circumstances."

"I am but it doesn't solve anything. If this was just a fight over a woman, we'd forget all about it. But it goes a lot deeper than that."

He ran a hand through his hair distractedly. So softly that she could barely hear him, he said, "He thinks I had a hand in the kidnapping."

She shivered. The day, though warm and sunny, seemed suddenly bleak. "Did you?"

Richard shot her a quick look. "You really are a change for James. He always liked pretty, compliant women, the way most of us do, I suppose. But you don't pull any punches."

"You're the one who keeps bringing it up. Obviously you want to talk about it. But it's James you should be discussing this with, not me."

"James won't discuss it. He isn't 'in' to me. His gargoyle of a secretary obviously has her instructions and so does everyone else. I've still got my office and even my title—for the moment—but otherwise I'm completely cut off. I've got no way to get through to him. Believe me, I've tried." Quietly, he added, "Which is where you come in."

"I barely know your brother," Kristina said hastily. Never mind the part of her that felt as though she had known him forever. The reality was that he was almost a stranger to her, a man who made her feel confused and even threatened in ways she didn't begin to understand. He had turned her emotions upside down and filled her with longings she had barely been aware of before. If she had any sense, she would run in the opposite direction.

But that was not what Richard was asking.

"All I want is for him to hear me out. I deserve that at least. You can convince him to do it, I know you can. Don't tell me you won't try."

"You don't know what you're asking."

"A chance, that's all."

"Your brother has been through one of the most terrible experiences any human being can know. He had his life taken away from him. Anyone would have trouble dealing with that but for him it's especially difficult because he won't admit how much he suffered. Admitting how frightened he was and how angry he still is are absolutely key to healing. The longer he delays doing that, the worse it will be. Something is bound to give and when it does . . ."

"All hell will break loose," Richard murmured.

Kristina nodded. She thought of James's extraordinary will, the driving strength and ruthlessness of his nature, and shivered. "I know it sounds cowardly, but when that happens, I'd just as soon not be in the line of fire."

"I can't blame you," Richard said wearily. "In your place I'd feel the same. After all, it's not as though you had any reason to care."

But she did, Kristina thought a short time later when they had parted company outside the park. Like it or not, she already cared far too much. She had gone to Innishffarin seeking truths about the past only to find that the present had a claim on her she could not ignore.

She could at least try to talk to James about his brother. In all likelihood, the worst he would do was refuse to hear her. The real problem was that she didn't know what she could say. Richard hadn't actually told her he was innocent. In fact, he hadn't said that at all.

A cloud moved before the sun. She shivered again and walked faster.

Chapter 9

James raised a hand to his forehead. It came away damp. He cursed under his breath. His stomach was clenched and the fine hairs at the back of his neck prickled. Despite his best efforts, a feeling of profound unease was growing inside him.

He turned away from the computer screen and glanced at the room. Nothing in it had changed. His office was exactly as it had been five minutes before when he returned from yet another meeting—large, elegantly furnished, with a panoramic view of the city below. If it lacked the ornateness common to executive domains, it was because he had always preferred it that way.

During his four-year absence, nothing had been touched. The marble-and-glass tables, the stark leather chairs, the austere modern paintings, everything was exactly the same as on the day he'd departed on that last, ill-fated journey. Since his return, he had altered nothing except the computer system. That he had up-graded his first day back.

The office had always been a refuge for him, a sanctuary from the weight of history that imbued every breath at Wyndham and equally from the hustle and bustle of the successful business he ran. He could always retreat to it to gather his thoughts, plan strategy or simply recharge.

But no longer. His mouth tightened as the weight in his chest grew. Despite his ordeal, he was in the peak of good health—extensive medical exams following his release had assured him of that. No physical cause lay behind what he was experiencing. No doctor could cure it. He was alone, locked in a solitude as profound as that which he had known in the small, dank cell of his memory. There was no escape.

His hand slipped. The mug of coffee he had been drinking crashed to the floor. He stared at the dark stain spreading across the carpet, uncertain what it was or how it had gotten there.

The phone on his desk shrilled. He picked it up on the second ring.

"What?"

"Mr. Davies would like a few minutes with you, sir." His secretary's voice was calm, almost flat, but with what was for her a definite undertone of concern.

He smiled grimly. Verona Morrow was one more of the things that hadn't changed. His secretary for five years before Beirut, she had stayed on in some honorary position during his absence, essentially because no one had the nerve to fire her. Before he stepped off the elevator his first day back, she resumed her post as guardian of his office, his schedule and—wherever possible—his peace of mind.

"Not now," he said, dragging the words up through the dark, bewildering vise that seemed to be closing around him. All day he had been seeing people, listening to their problems, searching for solutions. The full burden of running the business lay on him, as it always had before, as he took it for granted it always would.

That was the job, one many other men would have done almost anything to have. He knew that, indeed had savored it in the past. But he was suddenly, fiercely resentful of all the demands, all the pressure, the constant, unending responsibility.

"Not now," he said again through teeth that were nearly clenched.

"Very good, sir."

The connection ended. He heard static on the line and slowly put the phone down. Staring out the window, he forced himself to breathe deeply. The sky beyond the high windows was crystalline blue. If he bent forward slightly, he could see the barges and tourist boats making their way along the river.

London lay at his feet, spread out in all its glory. Should he choose to do so, he could walk out of his office, out of the building, and go anywhere he pleased. There was no cell, no chains, no blindfold, no death lurking behind every corner. He was free.

Why couldn't he believe it?

Anger flared in him, almost washing out the fear. His fists clenched. He wanted to hit something, to smash, to obliterate, to find some physical release for the frustration eating away at him. In the cell, he had done that sometimes, striking his fists against the walls until they bled. It had availed him nothing then and it certainly would not now. Violence solved nothing. Pray God, if he had learned nothing else, he had learned that.

It was over. The end he had prayed for, hungered for, hung on for had actually happened. Why then did he still hurt so much? Why was he still trapped?

He leaned his head back against the chair and shut his eyes. It would stop, it had to. He wouldn't—couldn't—live like this. Blood drummed through his veins, propelled by a heart that was beating as though he had run miles. He could still feel the perspiration on his forehead. His breath was ragged but worse yet was the terrifying sense of panic that threatened to engulf him.

From that, there was no escape. He was slipping away from himself, falling down an endless pit into oblivion.

His eyes shot open. The windows he had been looking through moments before suddenly seemed miles away. He could not move, could hardly breathe. He was helpless.

The phone rang again. He grabbed hold of the sound as though to a lifeline and let it pull him at least partway back.

"I'm very sorry, sir," Mrs. Morrow said. "I know you don't want to be disturbed, but there is a young lady out here who is most insistent." Her voice was icy, making it clear this was not her fault, she had been forced to interrupt him against her better judgment and in complete violation of all the rules of decorum.

That in itself was most remarkable. Not the least of the formidable Mrs. Morrow's attributes was her ability to wither the most assertive executive with a single glance from ten yards away. People who prided themselves on their self-confidence tended to tiptoe around her.

Well aware of her nickname—The Gargoyle—she displayed a small plastic model of her namesake on her desk with steely pride. No one—absolutely no one— *forced* Verona Morrow to do anything.

"Send her in," James said. How could he not? No one could refuse so extraordinary a creature.

Besides, the distraction was already proving to be a blessing. He could move again and his heartbeat was slowing. The windows were back where they had always been. Only the memory lingered, taunting him with thoughts of next time.

He stood up and smoothed his hair. His hand shook slightly but he contrived not to notice. All his attention was on the door to his office. Even as it opened, he knew who would be on the other side. Instinct, or hope, informed him before his eyes beheld the glint of golden hair or the small, tentative smile that touched Kristina's mouth.

"Is this a bad time?" she asked.

He laughed, a shade too loudly, and came forward to meet her, perhaps a little faster than he needed to but there was no getting around it, he was damn glad she was there.

"No," he said, "as a matter of fact, your timing is perfect."

"I am sorry, sir," Mrs. Morrow said, injecting herself right behind Kristina. "I told Professor Mc-Ginnis you weren't to be disturbed, but she insisted."

"That's all right," he assured the older woman and almost laughed again at her shock. Such benevolence was not usual for him.

"I'll come back if you're busy," Kristina said. Her eyes scanned the desk and its assortment of open files, the computer, the bank of phones. Whatever determination had gotten her this far seemed to be fading fast.

"I was thinking of quitting early," he said and reached for his jacket.

"Sir?" Mrs. Morrow murmured. She could not have looked more surprised had the world been turned upside down. James Wyndham walking out of the office at midday? Going off with some young person who had quietly but relentlessly breached Mrs. Morrow's most experienced defenses? And that young person was someone who defied classification—not at all like the questionable young women with whom Mr. Wyndham had sometimes socialized in the pre-Beirut days but also not at all like the regal Tessa Westerloo of whom Mrs. Morrow had never actually approved.

Someone who fit no category, followed no rules, and who showed up where she was least expected. Which was not to say she was unwelcome. Quite the contrary.

"Cancel whatever I have on tap for the rest of the day," James said as he slipped his arms into his suit jacket.

"The MP from Leeds, sir," Mrs. Morrow said, not without a hint of desperation. "The Board of Trade representative, the gentleman from the *Financial Times*..."

"Cancel them," James reiterated. He looked again toward the windows and smiled. "It's too nice a day to be stuck inside." Over his shoulder, he added, "You might think of leaving early yourself, Mrs. Morrow. Wouldn't do you a bit of harm."

"I don't think she believed you," Kristina said as they were going down in the elevator. She felt absurdly happy and wasn't sure why. The impulse that had brought her to James's office was as awkward as it was compelling. She didn't know why she suddenly had to see him, only that she did.

For a moment, just as she walked into his office, she'd had the terrifying impression that he might be ill. But it was gone so quickly it might never have been. He looked perfectly well, relaxed, and above all, glad to see her. Whatever doubts she felt couldn't hold a candle to that. For the moment at least, she was determined to simply relax and enjoy his company.

"Do you really not have to get back?" she asked as they left the building.

"I'm the boss, remember?"

"I wouldn't dare to forget," she said and cast him a quick, teasing look.

He shook his head wryly. "Something's made you daring. Either it went very well this morning or very badly. Which was it?"

"Well," she said and realized with a start that she had put the meeting with the grant board out of her mind. It should have mattered a great deal but it did not.

"Then we should celebrate."

"I suppose so." She sounded doubtful, not because she wasn't happy but because she was thinking of how to bring up the subject of Richard. That called for diplomacy, at the very least. For the moment, it seemed wiser to wait.

"What would you like to do?" James asked. "Go somewhere for lunch? Go shopping? Play tourist? What appeals to you?"

He did, Kristina thought, but she was too wise to say it. Instead, she said, "I dragged you away from work. You ought to pick."

"I didn't exactly require dragging," he pointed out, "but if you'd rather I choose..." He glanced around at the legions of well-dressed men and women pouring past them, the darting taxis and careening buses, the endless bustle of the city going at full throttle. London in all its majesty, the city he had first seen as a small boy, fallen in love with and ultimately made his own. The city that felt suddenly claustrophobic, as though it could swallow him alive.

"Come on," he said and turned toward the river.

Chapter 10

"Are you sure this is legal?" Kristina asked. She was floating, pillowed in softness, beneath dappled sunlight. The small skiff they had rented bobbed gently in the water as James poled it along. He was not working strenuously, content as he was to merely drift along the riverbank where daffodils had begun to bloom.

"Always has been," he said. "Haven't you ever gone boating on the Thames before?"

She shook her head. "I thought it was the stuff of legends, that and commercials. It didn't occur to me people actually still did it."

They were a mile or so beyond Hampton Court which they had also reached by boat from the foot of Westminster Bridge. The palace beckoned with all its fabled charms but they resisted it, striking out instead for the small dock where the skiffs were rented. On the way, they picked up sandwiches and drinks from a snack stand. On weekends, the place would have been thriving but on a workday it was all but deserted. They poled down a small estuary and found they had it virtually to themselves.

"I should be wearing a long white dress, something gauzy and Edwardian," Kristina lamented, "and a wide-brimmed straw hat tied with voile. Not this dreadful suit I put on to impress the grant board."

In fact, it was a perfectly nice suit consisting of a linen skirt and jacket in bright mauve paired with a violet silk blouse. Several years before, when she realized she would need something to wear to meetings with people who were giving her money, she had chosen it over the drab "managerette" style then so popular—running shoes, sensible gray suits, and bow ties being inclined to give her indigestion. Since then, the suit had done yeoman duty. She decided it deserved an afternoon out.

"You look lovely," James said because he knew he ought to and because it was true. For good measure, he added, "And you damn well know it."

"You're just saying that to be nice."

"Why would I want to do that?"

"Because I'm letting you have all the fun."

"Oh?"

"Sure. I haven't suggested once that I get to do some of the poling even though it's obviously the best part of this. You haven't heard a peep out of me about that, have you?"

"Heaven save me from bashful women."

"Where, where?"

"Here," he said and tossed her the pole. "You work for a while. I'm going to have a nap."

"You realize you're putting your fate in my hands?" she said as she got up gingerly, holding the pole. He looked insufferably pleased with himself.

"Couldn't ask for better," he said and stretched out on the cushions, promptly closing his eyes.

Maddening man, Kristina thought as she pulled the pole through the water. They were moving with the current which made it easier than she'd expected. Actually, it was rather soothing. There was nothing much to think about and worry was impossible. She was free to study the man stretched out at her feet.

His eyes were closed. He had taken off his jacket, as she had done hers. His tie was loosened and the top-most button of his shirt was undone. He looked strong, sinewy, taut with power and yet relaxed. Utterly different from the man she had glimpsed when she opened the door to his office.

Perhaps she had imagined it but for a moment he had looked so... trapped. There was no other word. Like an animal hunted and caged, without hope. A chill ran through her, at odds with the bright day. She had known all along that he was trying to do the impossible, to walk away from the past and pretend it had never existed. What she had not known, not really, was what the cost would be.

He was finding out.

Her hands faltered on the pole. The skiff turned in toward the shore and bumped gently against the bank. James opened his eyes. "Lunch?"

She nodded, not trusting herself to speak. Sudden, ravenous hunger seized her. She was glad when he took over securing the boat. Alone, she walked up the bank and found a spot under a venerable willow tree. Some thoughtful soul had provided a roughly spun brown blanket along with the skiff. She spread it out and opened the lunch they'd brought.

By the time she was done, James joined her. For a while, they ate in silence punctuated only by the hum of insects and the flutter of birds in the surrounding trees. Finally, she leaned back, wiggled her toes and said, "It's hard to believe we're only a few miles away from one of the largest cities in the world."

"That's the best part about London. You can get out of it quickly."

She almost said, "You looked as though you needed to get out, back there in the office." But she stopped herself. His feelings were private. He had a right to that.

"Your secretary's very impressive," she said instead. "Did you know she has a reproduction of a gargoyle from the northeast corner of Notre Dame on her desk?"

"I knew the species, not the origin. You undermined her confidence. I'll have to do something to shore it back up."

"Was I really that bad, bursting in the way I did?"

He crumpled the paper his sandwich had come in, dropped it back into the bag and grinned. "You were . . . a surprise. But then you always are."

"I can't understand that," she said, shaking her head. "I've always thought of myself as completely predictable."

His eyebrows rose. "You spend most of your time living in the thirteenth century. That strikes you as normal?"

"I don't actually live there. I'm just visiting."

"Pardon me, that makes all the difference."

"It was a fascinating time," she said defensively.

"I'm sure it was. In fact, I wouldn't mind visiting myself." He spoke lightly, not really meaning what he said, but Kristina seized on it.

"Would you really?" Before he could reply, she went on. "You know, I've been thinking about that. Innishffarin belongs to you, after all, yet you've barely seen what we're doing there. I ought to be able to change that."

"It's all right," he assured her, thinking that he really had no desire to run around in chain mail and milk cows. No, that wasn't right. Chain mail was for knights, milking cows was for someone else.

"I'd like you to see it," she said, staring off into space. To him, she looked transfixed, as though peering into a world he knew little about but which held untold wonders.

He felt obscurely jealous and so he did what came naturally. Her waist was slim and supple against his arm. She stiffened when he touched her but offered no resistance. It was as it had been with them each time—sudden, explosive, heated and exquisite.

He kissed her long and lingeringly. She responded in kind, opening herself to him and holding nothing back. Her boldness delighted him even as it drove him further. There in the sylvan setting, sheltered by the long hanging branches of the tree, they were safe from all the world. Nothing mattered except each other.

Far in the back of his mind was the realization that he had never taken so long with a woman. Never had he waited so long, anticipated so much, held back to such a degree. Yet with her it seemed natural. He needed time and so did she. For him there was the sense that a part of himself was still lost and that because of that he was more uncertain than he had ever been in his life. For her there was the newness and a certain caution that he thought did her credit.

For the moment, he was content to wait. Not that it was easy. The drive to possess her was almost overwhelming. She was sunlight, beauty, life, all he had longed for in the long, dark years of despair.

He loved the high, firm curve of her breasts, the nipples swollen beneath his tongue. The silk blouse gave way easily and the filmy bra with it. She was like a supple willow in his hands, strong but fluid.

But she was more, a human being of spirit and intelligence, a woman of imagination and courage, unlike any he had ever known. There, on the good English earth beside the ever-running river, he might have made her his. But he held back, afraid that he could, through carelessness or simple ignorance, spoil this rare and precious beauty that had, all unaccountably, come within his reach.

He sat up slowly, bringing Kristina with him. She was flushed and disheveled, her cheeks warm and her eyes afire with an ancient light. Exactly as she ought to look, he thought with some satisfaction, and smiled grimly.

"I'm not sure we ought to be allowed out in public," he said.

"We're not," she pointed out on a thread of sound.

"Don't remind me." He stood, dusted the good English dirt off his trousers, and gestured toward the skiff. "We ought to be getting back."

She followed slowly, saying nothing, her thoughts purely her own. There was no talk of her taking the pole this time. He did the work, against the current, and brought them quickly back to Hampton Court.

On the way back to London, he said, "I have to stay a few more days."

She said, "I've stayed away long enough. I'll take the plane tomorrow."

"You don't like to fly," he pointed out.

"I'll manage," she said and looked away from him, out over the city, growing thicker and denser, closing in around them again. Like memory.

She hadn't mentioned Richard. Not a word about him had passed her lips. There was a good reason for that. Very simply, she was afraid. Whatever it was that was happening between her and James was fragile, tenuous, even dangerous. He needed to trust her but he did not. He didn't trust anyone just then, not even himself.

She had to wait. And more, she needed her own ground, somewhere she felt safe. Strong enough to confront pain and fear, memory and desire, past and future.

Innishffarin.

Chapter 11

She hardly remembered the plane ride to Edinburgh. She, who hated flying, took it in stride and thought nothing of it. Her thoughts were elsewhere.

The students had managed beautifully. The cows were milked, the goats fed, the floors swept and laid with fresh rushes, all was exactly as it should be.

She felt unneeded. Which was silly, of course, as her students were at pains to tell her. They had missed her, they said. They were delighted to hear how well everything had gone. They fairly overflowed with enthusiasm and youthful energy.

She felt old. Which was ridiculous since she was hardly that. But their lives seemed so uncomplicated when compared to the confusion of her own life. She missed James from the very moment that she left him, and she almost dreaded the moment when she would see him again.

She was confused. Well, that was life, wasn't it? Confusing, bewildering, frustrating, frightening, gloriously improbable life. Safe, it wasn't.

Her hand brushed the stones of the outer curtain wall and came away wet. It was raining again. Her work was finished, at least for the moment. The students were busy. She was alone. Linus beckoned.

She opened the illuminated manuscript reluctantly. No mention there of a sea cave, no clue as to how it might be reached. Nothing. She needed to care but she couldn't muster the strength. The wet, dank day drained her. She thought of James, as she did far too often, and frowned.

He was in London where she imagined the sun was shining. Not because she had any reason to think that it was, but she envisioned it that way. Which was worse? Envisioning him with someone a little warmer, a little more appealing than the frosty Tessa? Or alone? As he had been that moment in his office.

The carefully scripted words that she had studied so many times before meant nothing to her. She closed the book and stood up. There must be something she could find to occupy herself. She needed hard, exhausting work. The best she could do was walk along the beach.

Bundled up in an oiled wool cape with the hood pulled over her head, she made her way down the rocky path to the water's edge. Once there, she had second thoughts. There were few activities less suited to a soggy day but restlessness propelled her on. She dodged the tiny wavelets washing in with the tide and let her eye drift aimlessly along the edge of the cliff.

A few dauntless scrubs clung to the perpendicular expanse. Here and there mineral deposits stained the sand purple or black. With the sun obscured by clouds, there were no shadows. But it was almost possible to see them all the same, clinging to the shallow depressions and hidden places that etched the surface of the cliff, almost as though...

She stopped and stared. There, high up along the cliff, surely she must be imagining that small square of darkness? It was too regular to be a mineral deposit, too flat to be a bush. What was it exactly?

She drew closer, her eyes narrowed. Above her, the cliff rose proud and indomitable. Above it, set a little way into the shore, was the outermost wall of Innishffarin itself. She was standing directly beneath the castle. Two-thirds of the way up the cliff the small square beckoned. It looked almost like...no it couldn't be...a window?

In the side of a cliff? Her imagination was running away with her. She was tired, preoccupied, and seeing things. That was all there was to it. Cliffs did not have windows. Everyone knew that.

Yet this one did. The more she looked at it, the more convinced she became. Someone, in some far distant time, had carved an opening in the cliff. Perhaps that person had climbed up from the beach or perhaps he had come from the other side. From the castle.

James had said the Wyndham Cross was found in a sea cave by the side of the cliff. The entrance had long since been sealed off. Or had it? Was it even remotely possible that there had been more than one way in?

She was crazy to even think of it. There was no assurance that a window actually existed, it might be only a trick of the lighting. But if it was real... She had no experience climbing and could easily be hurt trying to scale the cliff. If she had any sense at all, she would forget all about it.

Except that she couldn't, try though she did, through all the rest of that day and the next. The image of the tiny square of darkness set in the cliff side kept returning to taunt her. She had to find a way to reach it.

And indeed, as is usually the case with those things that are most desired, a solution did finally present itself.

It happened by accident.

She came back into the castle bailey, discouraged, with her mind on what else she might do to keep herself occupied. Hardly anyone was about. The wet weather had driven everyone inside, except for Standish who was sitting under an overhang by the stable door, playing with a length of rope.

"What's that?" she asked.

"A way to pass the time," he said, looking a little sheepish. He held up the rope for her examination. "I'm tying knots."

"Whatever gets you through the day."

He laughed. "It's not as bad as it looks. These are climbing knots. You use them for rappeling down mountainsides."

"Maybe you do. I prefer to keep my feet on the ground..." She broke off, staring at him. "What did you say?"

"Rappeling. It's a technique where you use the thrust of your body swinging at the end of a rope to lever yourself up or down a slope. Works pretty well if you know what you're doing."

"You're a rock climber," she said as though she had suddenly discovered the most marvelous thing about him. As indeed she had, or more correctly, remembered it. The résumé he'd presented to win his place in the group had mentioned rock climbing as a hobby.

"I fool around a little," he admitted modestly.

"More than that. You climbed that mountain in Alaska, what's it called?"

"Mount McKinley. It wasn't such a big deal."

"You got to the top, didn't you? And more importantly, you got back down to the bottom. Right?"

Slowly, he nodded. "So?"

"So you'd be able to help someone climb a little itty-bitty cliff, right?"

He frowned, cautious of whatever it was that might be coming. "That would depend."

"On what?"

"On how itty, how bitty, and who the someone was."

"I'm the someone and the cliff is right around back. It's hardly anything at all. You could probably do it in your sleep."

"Maybe," he conceded, "but why would I want to?"

"You wouldn't, but I would. In fact, I want it very much. What do you say, can you help me?"

He put the rope down and looked at her long and hard. "It's not as easy as you might think. Even small climbs can be dangerous, especially for amateurs."

"I'll take the risk."

"Okay, but that doesn't mean I will. Why do you want to climb the cliff?"

"To see what's at the top."

"Excuse me, but there's an easier way to do that. Just walk on back behind the castle and look."

"All right," she conceded, "not all the way to the top. There's an anomaly in the cliff face about two-thirds of the way up. I want to find out what's causing it."

Frank frowned. He looked interested but hesitant. "I wasn't aware we were doing a geological survey along with everything else."

"We aren't. This has possible historical significance." She hesitated, reluctant to say more but also realizing that she'd have to. "There's a chance—only a chance, mind you—that the Wyndhams buried something in the cliff. Obviously, it would be futile to search the entire expanse on either side of the castle. But I did happen to notice this anomaly and I'd really like to take a look."

"Two-thirds of the way up?"

She nodded.

"That's about a hundred, maybe a hundred and twenty feet, and the cliff is pretty sheer. Are you sure they buried something up there?"

"No. As I said, it's only a chance."

He stood, stretched, and stared out at the rain. "It won't be easy. Maybe it would be better if I just went up and took a look."

"I'm sure it would be but this is kind of my baby, going up is my idea. If something happened to you, I'd blame myself."

"I'm hardly as likely as you are to have a problem," he pointed out.

"Still, I'd feel safer if you were on the ground, telling me what to do."

He fell silent again and she thought for a moment that he was going to refuse. But finally he shrugged and picked up the rope again. "You're the teacher. Besides, it's your hide. When do you want to do this?"

"Now isn't good?"

"Not on your life. Maybe tomorrow if the weather dries out."

"Tomorrow," she said and felt a little thrill of excitement. "Is there anything I should do in the meantime?"

He shook his head. "Sprout wings if you can. Otherwise, get a good night's sleep and leave the rest to me." As she turned to go, he added, "And wear something sensible. We'll be using twentieth-century climbing techniques, not thirteenth. Okay?"

That was fine with her. Now that she'd won his agreement, reality was beginning to set in. The thought of what she would actually have to do made her a little queasy. Twice in the night she awoke to the sound of the rain and thought she might be reprieved. But dawn broke bright and sunny, and the cliff side awaited.

"Easy," Frank shouted as he pulled the rope taut. "Do it just like we practiced, nice and slow. That's it, better. You've got it now. Keep your arms straight and dig your feet in."

Kristina breathed in deeply. The muscles in her arms ached, her heart was beating fast, and she felt faintly dizzy. But she was also making progress. Very slow progress, to be sure, but progress all the same.

For a moment, she was tempted to glance down but common sense intervened. "Whatever you do," Frank had warned her, "don't look down. Later on, when you're more experienced, that will be fun but right now all it will do is scare the daylights out of you. Keep your eyes straight ahead or slightly raised. Got it?''

She had assured him that she did, just as she had done her best to absorb all the other instructions he had given her in the several hours of training that preceded the actual climb. There was some comfort in the fact that everything was pretty straightforward. You did this and this and this because if you didn't, gravity would take over and you'd be dead. Simple. Also easy to remember when the stakes were your life.

She could do this, she told herself. She *was* doing it. All she had to do was keep her mind on her objective and she'd be fine.

She looked up, locating the dark square in the cliff side. It was harder to see now because the sun cast shadows that partly obscured it. That worried her. What if she'd only imagined what she'd thought she'd seen the previous day? What if her desire to find the rest of the Wyndham Treasure was so great that it was playing tricks with her mind?

Nonsense, she'd seen what she'd seen and with a little effort, she'd be able to reach it. The thought of what she might discover there spurred her on. She rappeled out again from the side of the cliff, swinging at the end of the rope Frank had rigged from the top. On the return swing, her feet connected with the sandy surface. The force swung her out again. At the same time, she pulled upward on the rope. The combination of outward and upward thrust worked together to raise her farther than she could have managed with one move alone.

After the initial shock, the process became almost matter-of-fact. There was a certain rhythm to it that made sense. As long as she didn't let herself think too much about what she was doing, she was fine.

The students gathered below seemed to think so, too. They cheered as she completed one particularly long loop out and back. It hadn't been her intention to have an audience but once word spread of what she and Frank were up to, there was no holding them back. The best she could say was that none of them was laying bets as to whether she'd make it. At least, she didn't think anyone was.

Another loop, another few feet. The distance to the ground was widening. Don't look down, her mind said, just as her head was about to turn in that direction. She fought the impulse and kept going.

There, above her in the sunlight, that was it. Wasn't it? She could make out a distinct square of darkness against the lighter cliff side—more of a rectangle actually now that she looked at it more closely. Set deep and with no light showing beyond, but there nonetheless. It could simply be a crevice, she knew that. But the shape appeared to be man-made, nature not being inclined to work in right angle corners.

Another fifty feet or so, maybe slightly more, and she would be there. Her hands tightened on the rope. Eagerness filled her.

"Easy," Frank shouted from the ground. "You're doing fine but don't speed up. Keep the rhythm."

She took another deep, steadying breath and forced herself to be calm. There was no rush, she could take her time and get there quickly enough. Never mind that her arms throbbed from the unaccustomed strain. It wasn't much farther. Soon, very soon, she would be . . .

The sound of horse's hooves pounding down the beach broke her concentration. She hesitated.

Don't look down.

"What the bloody hell's going on?" an angry voice demanded. James's voice, incredulous and enraged. From the stallion's back, he surveyed the scene disbelievingly—the students gathered beside the cliff, Standish holding the rope, and swinging from it, suspended in mid-air, none other than . . .

The gray horse shied, feeling the tension in his master. His front legs lifted, hooves pawing the air.

James cursed under his breath and pulled taut on the reins, controlling the animal quickly. But the damage was already done. Several of the students cried out reflexively, a handful scattered. Frank, holding the rope, did not move, but his hands loosened. The tension eased, just enough to knock Kristina off balance.

She swung wildly and slammed into the cliff side. The breath was knocked from her. Desperately, she tried to hold on even as Frank shouted to her not to let go. Too late. A hundred feet in the air above the rock-strewn beach, she lost her grip and plummeted toward the ground.

Chapter 12

The safety rope stopped her. Without it, she would have fallen a hundred feet to serious injury, at the least. As it was, she came away with nothing more than a few bruised ribs and a sense of having run her luck out about as far as any reasonable person would ever want to.

James saw it differently. He looked at the bruised and limp body being lowered to the ground and knew a spurt of terror more profound than any he had ever experienced in Beirut or afterward. Very simply, he felt as though someone had torn a hole in the world, or at least tried to.

"You bloody idiot," he said to Frank whose role in the escapade he had no trouble discerning. "What in hell were you thinking of to let her go up there?"

"She wanted to," Frank said, not unreasonably. For good measure, he added, "She was doing fine until you came along."

He took a quick step back when he saw the expression on James's face. "I'm not saying it was your fault, it wasn't. But you've got to understand, she's the teacher, she's in charge here. When she said she wanted to climb the cliff, I couldn't really tell her no."

James shook his head in disgust. He turned away from the younger man and bent over Kristina. She was pale and looked in pain, but she managed a faint smile.

"Don't be mad at him. It was my fault."

"You're right," he said gruffly. "You need your head examined, but first..." He ran his hands quickly, almost expertly over her, judging the extent of her injuries. "You were lucky," he murmured when he had reassured himself they were not severe.

Kristina said nothing. She was too busy thinking about the effect his touch had on her. There she was, battered and bruised, having just all but fallen off the side of a cliff and all the man had to do was touch her to send her senses spinning into orbit. She started to shake her head, realized that it hurt too much, and stopped.

James lifted her effortlessly into his arms. He stood, feet planted firmly apart, and glared at the others. "You may think she's in charge but the land is mine and I won't stand for this kind of foolishness. Get that gear off the cliff and get yourselves back to work. If there's any more trouble from any of you, you'll answer to me."

That had the desired effect. No one stayed to argue. The ropes were packed away with lightning speed and the students dispersed to their various tasks. Frank did linger for a moment but a dark scowl from the laird sent him quickly on his way.

"Can you ride?" James asked.

"Ride what?" Kristina murmured. She was beginning to feel light-headed, though whether from her near escape or from the man himself she couldn't say. "A merry-go-round, a painted pony, what did you have in mind?"

He made a sound deep in his throat and turned toward the gray stallion which stood patiently nearby. "You need a keeper," he said as he settled her as gently as possible into the saddle. Kristina winced but didn't argue. Nobody with a gnat's worth of sense would have disagreed with the laird of Innishffarin just then.

"You're supposed to be in London," she murmured as he swung up behind her and reached around to take the reins.

"I came back."

"Why?"

"Because I did. Now be quiet. We'll be at Wyndham as quickly as I can manage it."

"Wyndham? I don't want to go there. Just take me back up to the castle. I'll be fine."

"If you think I'm leaving you injured in that pile of stones with those idiots to look after you, you need to think again. Now be a good girl and close your mouth. You don't want flies getting in."

He was a throwback, Kristina decided, a remnant of that unlamented era before men realized that women were independent beings capable of making their own decisions. A chauvinist, patronizing, insufferable, arrogant.

None of which explained why she was willing to lean back against his broad chest, close her eyes and let the soothing motion of the gray stallion carry her away.

Careful though James was to keep the horse to a slow pace, by the time they reached Wyndham, Kristina was feeling the worse for wear. Her ribs hurt and her legs felt weak. All too easily, she felt again the sickening plunge as her hands gave way and the ground rushed up toward her.

Yet, she remembered too, how close she had come to her objective and couldn't help but regret that it had been snatched from her.

In the confusion following her fall, no one had mentioned the "anomaly" that had sent her up the cliff side in the first place. For that she was grateful. James was angry enough as it was. She didn't want to know how he would react if he discovered she'd been in search of something he considered to be a myth.

In fact, she didn't want to think of anything at all.

It was so much easier to just lie back and let him take charge. Cowardly, perhaps, and in the long run not a terribly good idea. But for the moment, the temptation proved irresistible.

She supposed it was because at heart she was a romantic.

How many chances did a girl get to be carried up the curving marble steps of a grand manor, down a hallway lined with ancestral portraits, and deposited in a high, four-poster bed, all by a very large, very determined male who seemed to think she ought to do exactly what he said and be glad he was around to say it?

Not enough, that was how many. Perhaps she'd struck her head against the side of the cliff and hadn't realized it. Certainly, she wasn't feeling herself.

Far in the back of her mind, a small voice muttered about caution and common sense but Kristina couldn't quite focus on it. It was so much nicer to sink back against the down-filled pillows and watch James as he went around the room closing the curtains.

"I'll call the doctor," he said as he returned to the bed. Deftly, he removed her boots and dropped them on the floor. She was left in jeans and an old plaid shirt. Her hair had come loose from the beret she'd put it in. It spilled over the pillows and around her shoulders. She looked up at him, unaware that her eyes were slumberous with unspoken thoughts.

"Do you have to go?" she asked.

"Yes," James said huskily. "I rather think I do. You're not quite yourself."

She giggled, a most amazing sound for a woman who had always prided herself on her self-possession. "I was just thinking the same thing. Who do you suppose I am?"

"Some glorious daft creature who thinks she can fly?" he suggested.

She shook her head mournfully. "I tried last night to grow wings but it didn't work."

James frowned. "How many of me are you seeing exactly?"

"Just one and that's quite enough, thank you. More than enough in fact. I don't really know what to do with you."

He looked amused at the notion. "That's up to you to decide, is it?"

"Maybe not," she admitted. "I don't have much practice at this kind of thing."

"Really? I wouldn't have guessed."

"I hide it pretty well."

"In fact, you don't hide it at all but that doesn't matter. Close your eyes."

"I can't," she said and reached for his hand. "I'm afraid I'll fall."

James sighed under his breath. "Aren't we all?"

He sat down on the edge of the bed, her hand in his. The doctor would have to wait. Very simply, he couldn't bear to leave her, not even for a few minutes. The image of her plummeting down the side of the cliff was burned into his brain.

He thought again of Standish, briefly regretted letting him go so easily, and sighed. Had he really thought life was complicated before? He'd had no real idea of how confusing and enticing it could become when the right woman happened along.

His eyes, ice blue as the northern sky, widened slightly. Right woman? Where had that come from? She was an intrusion, a complication, an irritation and a frustration. There was nothing at all right about her.

Not unless he counted the trusting way her hand nestled in his, the small but delightful pout of her soft lips, the delicate bloom of color on her cheeks, the supple and strong body concealed at the moment by those dreadful clothes.

Nothing at all.

This was a joke of sorts, he decided. A cosmic flight of fancy intended to demonstrate to him that whatever else life would be, it would never turn out the way he expected. With all he'd been through, he shouldn't need to be reminded of that.

He sighed again and lifted his legs onto the bed. She murmured and moved closer without opening her eyes. Carefully, he put an arm around her shoulders. Her breathing was deep and regular; she no longer appeared to be in pain.

Maybe the doctor wasn't really needed after all. Maybe nothing was needed except this quiet gentle intimacy, so delicate that he was afraid a mere gust of wind might blow it away.

But the curtains were closed, blotting out the day, sealing them within a private world. For the moment, it was enough.

"Is there anything else you'll be needing, miss?" the maid asked.

Kristina shook her head a little dazedly. What else could any human being possibly ever need? She was back in the same guest room she had used before, having awakened there a short while ago. The curtains were pulled but she could tell that night had fallen. So, too, did she gather from the rumpled bedclothes beside her that she had not been alone all that time.

Nor was she alone now. The maid had arrived almost as soon as she opened her eyes, as though summoned by some secret signal. She brought a tray of raspberry tea—very soothing, she said—a liniment for her bruised ribs that worked wonders, and a nononsense air that made it clear things were going to be done right.

For starters, there was the bath. Kristina had contemplated a bracing hot shower before climbing back into her wrinkled clothes and setting off back to Innishffarin. The maid had other ideas.

"A good long soak, that's what you need," she informed Kristina as she bustled into the marble and gilt bathroom, obviously added long after the manor's construction and updated several times since. As large as some dormitory bedrooms Kristina had occupied

during her student days, the bath was the last word in
sybaritic pleasure.

The tub was huge, with spray jets and a padded neck
rest. Music played softly from an invisible stereo.
There was even a fire in the—yes, the fireplace. All
that and a heated rack holding oversize towels with
fluff to drown in, not to mention an array of appropriately scented bath crystals from which to select.

"Honeysuckle, I think," she said when queried on
this point by the maid. She tried to make it sound as
though this were a decision she made every day but
wasn't sure she quite pulled it off.

Not to mind. The maid—young enough to be one of
Kristina's students but decades older in manner—
merely nodded, dumped in the appropriate amount,
gave the water a swirl and departed, with one final reminder that should Kristina need anything further she
had only to press the small white button within easy
reach of the tub.

"I'll do that," she promised although she couldn't
imagine anything that would prompt her to take such
an action. A whim for chamomile rather than raspberry tea? A preference for a different sort of liniment? An inability to decide which towel was best?

Did people really live this way, so pampered that all
the concerns of ordinary life seemed part of a different world? And if they did, however did they manage
to go back out in that world and cope as James did
and Richard, too, after his own fashion?

She had a suspicion what the answer might be and
didn't like it. The lairds of Innishffarin had long had
a reputation for cosseting their women. They tended
to be bold and aggressive men, given to taking what-

ever happened to seize their eye. But once married, they held true.

No complaints from Wyndham women had made their way down through the ages. Which wasn't to say there hadn't been any. Living with those oversize males endowed with the mistaken belief that they knew best about everything couldn't have been easy. It must have taken an indomitable woman to stand up to one of them. Fortunately, the family seemed to attract exactly that.

She sank down into the water cautiously. It was hot and stung at first but she got used to it quickly enough. The fogginess that had plagued her since awakening eased somewhat. She put out a hand, found the tea placed carefully on a low table beside the tub, and took a sip. Like everything else, it was perfect.

The events of the morning, the struggle up the cliff, her sudden fall, all seemed part of the distant past. Only this was real. Until, that is, she finished the tea and the bath water began to cool. Reluctantly, she stood up, wrapped herself in one of the oversize towels, and went back into the bedroom.

While she was in the tub, the maid had lit the lamps. They filled the room with rose-hued light. She looked around, half expecting to find a silk and lace peignoir or something equally enticing but there was nothing. Telling herself that was for the best, she slipped her clothes back on, ran a brush through her hair, and went out into the hall.

It was deserted but she could hear voices far below. Following them, she found James ensconced in a room off the central hall, the library. He had the television on.

"There you are," he said when he saw her and stood, clicking the TV off at the same time. "Feeling better?"

"Some," she admitted, hoping she didn't sound as perturbed as she felt. It was silly really but she had expected...what? Firelight and honeysuckle, night-wrapped mystery and perhaps, just perhaps, very proper British seduction, presuming there was such a thing.

"I ordered supper in here," he said. "Soup and sandwiches. I hope that's all right."

She assured him that it was and went over to stand by the fire. One thing had to be said for these old manors, they had fireplaces everywhere the builder could think to put one.

"I'll drive you back when we're done," he said, "since you seem no worse for wear. But I want you to promise me something first."

The sun, the moon and the stars? she thought.

"You won't try anything like that again," he said.

She repressed a sigh. He was being so rigidly sensible. Had she been mistaken in what she thought she'd seen in his eyes during those moments when he held her so gently on the bed, right before she slipped into sleep? Obviously so, for he seemed now like nothing more than a good host, reasonably concerned that a guest on his property not come to any harm.

"I promise," she said and was relieved when Butler Berkowitz appeared at the open door carrying a well-laden tray.

"Supper sir?" he inquired after giving her a polite nod of the head.

"On the table there," James directed.

As he placed the various plates, bowls and glasses appropriately, the butler said, "By the way, sir, Mr. Richard called again."

When James made no comment but merely picked up a bottle of claret and studied the label, Bernard Berkowitz added, "He seems most anxious to speak with you, sir."

"You told him I was busy?"

"As you instructed, sir."

"Then he ought to be satisfied with that."

"If you say so, sir." On that note, Butler Berkowitz departed. Only the slightest lift of his eyebrows suggested that he not only disagreed with his employer but thought his actions ill-advised.

"Would you care to sit down?" James asked as he held out a chair for her.

Kristina did so, then waited as he joined her. They were sitting close enough to the fire to feel the heat of it but not so close as to be uncomfortable. The perfect compromise, she thought, and smiled.

"Something amuses you?" James asked as he poured wine for them both.

"Only the unlikeliness of all this."

He was silent for a moment before smiling suddenly in a way that seemed to strip ten years off his age. She had a brief, piercing glimpse of the boy he had been before time and experience conspired to rob him of such ease.

"It takes some getting used to, doesn't it?" he asked.

"Or getting used to again," she replied, rather pointedly, she thought. But then, no one had ever accused her of being subtle.

His smile faded. She could almost feel him withdrawing and regretted her haste. They ate in silence for several minutes. The soup was asparagus flavored with mint, the sandwiches were thick slices of fresh-baked bread with chunks of still warm roast chicken between them. Bernard Berkowitz might be the last word in butlers but he knew plenty of homespun comforts.

Finally, because one of them had to say something and she was afraid it was going to be him, she took a deep breath and jumped.

"I saw Richard when I was in London."

James looked up. Nothing in his expression gave away his thoughts, nor did his voice. "Did you?"

"Outside the grant board. We ran into each other."

"Really?"

"Look," she said, a touch exasperated, "he's your brother. Try to sound at least a little interested."

"Is there any particular reason why I should?"

"He cares about you."

James gave a short, harsh laugh. "You can't be that naive."

"Want to bet?" Kristina muttered. She was seriously in over her head on this one. The plunge off the cliff was nothing by comparison. But once she'd started she couldn't see any way to stop. Not if she was going to live with her conscience.

"All he wants is to talk with you."

"We have talked."

"About something other than the time of day."

James put his napkin down and leaned back in his chair, his long legs stretched out in front of him. The top buttons of his shirt were undone. His hair looked as though he'd been running his fingers through it, as usual. She was used to seeing him impeccably groomed but now he looked as though he needed a shave. His lean jaw was clenched. He looked very tired.

"Look," she said softly, "this is none of my business but..."

"You're right about that at least."

She ignored the pointed jab and pushed on. "It just seems to me that some things can't be avoided. All he wants is a chance to make his case."

"And what case is that?" James asked. "The case for why I lost four years of my life? Is that what I'm supposed to listen to my brother tell me?"

The deadly rage in his voice stabbed through Kristina. Before she could reply, he stood up abruptly and walked to the far end of the library.

Standing in shadows, all but invisible to her, he said, "When I was twelve years old, and Richard was ten, he came adventuring with me. That's what we called it back then. I was the big brother showing him the way, rather taken with myself to tell the truth. But Richard fixed that. He waited until we were near the river, gave me a good push and sent me flying. It was funny as far as he was concerned but unfortunately my head hit a rock and I was knocked out. I would have drowned if a poacher hadn't spotted me."

"What did your parents say to that?"

"Nothing. I never told them, and the poacher certainly wasn't about to. As for Richard, he did his damnedest to pretend nothing happened."

"He isn't doing that now."

"He'd be smarter if he was."

She stood and went to him. When she was still some little distance away, she asked, "Did you ever go adventuring together after that?"

A bittersweet smile touched his mouth. "We did."

"Then you still trusted him."

"No," James said quietly, "I can't say that I did."

Kristina shivered inwardly. If he hadn't trusted his brother, then who did he trust? Only himself, apparently. But that solitary and self-sufficient individual, that indomitable and essentially untouchable person was gone, shattered beyond recovery in the pain and horror of Beirut. And that left . . . no one . . .

"I watched my back," James said implacably, "until one day I foolishly got careless."

"You don't know that he . . ."

"I didn't exactly publicize the fact that I was traveling to Beirut. In fact, I kept it very close. There were diplomatic reasons. We had British hostages in Lebanon. It seemed that I had a chance to be of some help but instead . . ." He broke off, his eyes fathomless.

On impulse, she reached out to him. Her hand brushed his cheek lightly. Beneath the shadowed growth of beard, his skin was cold.

He seized her hand, tight in his own. Very softly, he said, "You should not be here."

"But I am," she replied and went into his arms.

Chapter 13

His hand shook slightly as he stroked the slender line of her back, so delicate yet so strong beneath his touch. He could smell the perfume of her hair evoking memories of sun-drenched summer days. Her skin was satin smooth, warm velvet and cream tinged with rose. Beneath the rough clothes she wore, he felt the heat of her body reaching out to him.

She was lovely, real, infinitely appealing, and there. Right there in his arms, in the solitude of the fire-lit room, far from all the world. Yet still he hesitated. From that first moment of meeting, he had desired her. She touched him in a way no woman had ever done. With her, the need that had always been a controllable source of pleasure and diversion became something else altogether.

He felt his hand shake and grimaced. He had never been so close to the edge before. For the first time in his life, he had to consider the possibility that he might physically hurt a woman.

The idea horrified him. He took a quick step back and shook his head. "You should go."

Kristina's eyes widened. Granted, she didn't think of herself as exactly a woman of the world but surely this was unusual? Unless she had misread everything from the beginning, he wasn't "immune to her charms," as her mother would have said. Far from it. So why was he behaving like this? "James . . . ?"

"I'll get Bernie to drive you back." He couldn't trust himself with her in the car; he'd already found that out.

"All right," she said slowly and stepped away from him. Her face was hot and she felt vaguely ill. What a fool she'd made of herself. He was sophisticated, worldly, a man who undoubtedly always expected to make the first move. And the last.

She'd blown it, plain and simple. Back to her medieval manuscript and her cow mulch. That's where she belonged. Not here in a gilded manor house trying to seduce a man as far removed from her own world as the stars might be.

"You're an idiot," James said. He was smiling suddenly, a wry smile to be sure and accompanied by yet another shake of his head. But a smile all the same.

"Probably," she murmured stiffly. "Good night."

"Not so fast," his hand reached out, closing gently but firmly around her arm.

"It's the most remarkable thing," he said, drawing her toward him. "I've suddenly discovered that I'm telepathic. Either that or you are."

"I have no idea what you're . . ."

"You, me, and the misbegotten thoughts swirling through your head. That's what I'm talking about." More seriously, he added, "Has it occurred to you that I may not be the best person for you to get to know just now?"

"No," she said honestly. "Why would I think that?"

He sighed, his eyes looking heavenward as though the ornately molded ceiling might hold a clue to divine revelation. "Let me explain it to you," he said. His fingers curled around her chin, tipped her head back so that her eyes met his. "To put it bluntly, sex was always something I took for granted without taking it very seriously. Not that I was careless; you'd have to be crazy to be that. But it was in the same category as a good meal or a satisfying workout. Just a normal part of life."

Her color deepened. She looked away. "I guess we see things differently."

"Wait," he said. "When I was in Beirut, there were plenty of things I missed and that was one of them, but I was mostly concerned with staying alive. Nothing else came even close."

"I can understand that."

"Good. Now here's the problem." He paused for a moment. A pulse beat in his jaw. Belatedly, she realized that he had himself rigidly in check, as though he feared what might happen if he let his control slip even for a second. "You're a very beautiful woman," he said quietly, "and a very special one. I don't want to hurt you."

Kristina took a quick, sharp breath. "I see . . ."

"Do you?" His hand tightened around her waist. He moved just enough to bring her body against his.

Her thighs brushed his. She gasped softly. His arousal was unmistakable. They were barely touching yet he was fully ready to possess her.

"It shouldn't be like this," he said, his breath warm against her throat. "You deserve candlelight and music, patience and great care. I'm not capable of that right now." He laughed harshly. "I may never be again, at least not where you're concerned. Before we both regret it, go."

She intended to, really. Every particle of sense she possessed told her to turn around and walk out of that room immediately. She'd had fair warning. Nothing could have been clearer. To stay was to invite more trouble than she was capable of handling.

But to go, to leave him as he was . . . she simply couldn't bring herself to do it.

"I've got a better idea," she said and smiled.

"This isn't a game, Kristina."

"Oh, I know that. In fact, it's very serious and so am I." A wild sense of daring filled her. She was swinging off the cliff again, floating free in space, risking everything on the chance—just the chance— that she wouldn't tumble. "Let's make a bet," she said.

He exhaled sharply and turned away from her. "Kristina . . ."

"I want you to talk with Richard. In fact, I think it's very important but you don't want to do it. So let's make a bet. If I win, you at least hear him out. If I lose, you do whatever you want."

He turned back and looked at her narrowly. "And the stakes?"

"Your self-control. You don't trust yourself, I do. Let's find out who's right." He stared at her for a long moment before he shook his head disbelievingly. "You don't know what you're saying."

"Yes, I do," she assured him softly. Before he could stop her, she lifted both her hands to his face and cupped it gently. The skin was warm and rough beneath her touch. The bristle of a day's growth of beard made her palms tingle.

"Besides," she said huskily, "you've got nothing to worry about. I have very little experience at this sort of thing. Resisting me ought to be a breeze."

"And if it isn't?"

"Think of that long talk you'll have to have with your brother."

He grimaced. "This comes under the category of hitting a man when he's down."

"I never said I played fair," she said. Ignoring the fluttering in her stomach, she raised herself on tiptoe and lightly brushed her mouth against his. He remained unmoving.

"Not bad," she said. "See how easy it'll be?"

"You're crazy, a beautiful loon. We both know what you're doing here and it isn't right. If you had more experience, you'd realize how vulnerable you can be."

"I'll take the risk," she said and stepped back to study him. The prospect before her was formidable. Granted, he was fully aroused but he was also determined not to give in to it. She had virtually no experience in seducing a man. Where to begin?

At the beginning, where else?

"You have beautiful eyes," she said gravely.

He couldn't help it, he laughed. It wasn't that he wanted to hurt her feelings, far from it. But the whole situation was preposterous and growing more so by the moment.

"Kristina . . ."

Uh, oh, not so preposterous after all. She took advantage of that laugh to come close again, running her hands lightly down his chest and breathing ever so softly on the bare burnished skin near the base of his neck. His stomach clenched. She was a beautiful, crazy innocent who had no idea of what she was doing. It was up to him to protect her. He'd give her a few more minutes, just enough for her to realize that she wasn't going to succeed, and then he'd send her packing.

Just a few more minutes . . .

Her mouth touched his again. So lightly that he could barely feel it, the tip of her tongue explored his lips.

He closed his eyes against the sweetly stabbing pleasure and told himself this was nothing. He had known far more accomplished women and had always remained fully in control. She was a novice. There was nothing she could do. But the pounding of his blood and the tightening in his loins said differently. When she stepped away, a tremor of disappointment rocked him. But she didn't go far and she didn't wait long. Artlessly, she tossed her head, sending a shower of golden hair over her shoulders. Firelight danced in her eyes as she fingered the buttons of his shirt.

Slowly, she undid the first button and the next. Her forehead furrowed in concentration. "Hold still," she warned. "I don't want to do this wrong."

"You're managing so far," he muttered and thrust his hands deep into the pockets of his trousers.

She pulled the shirt free of his waistband. One by one, the buttons gave way. When the last of them was free, she slipped her hands beneath the cool, finely woven fabric and touched his heated skin.

The tiny moan she gave was easily the most sensuous sound he had ever heard. She pressed her palms flat against him and moved them slowly up and down his chest.

Her breath quickened. She swallowed hard and managed a smile. "You feel wonderful."

He closed his eyes, fighting for control. "Didn't your mother ever tell you not to say things like that?"

"Well, let's see now," she murmured as her fingers found his flat male nipples. "She said to always carry a handkerchief, never drink anything stronger than sherry, and make sure I knew my own mind. That was about it."

"A wise woman, your mother," he said huskily.

She made an incoherent sound of agreement and spread the shirt farther. Beneath, his chest was broad, the burnished skin stretched taut over powerful muscles. Dark swirls of hair spread between his nipples and down in a furred line that disappeared into his pants.

Hardly aware of what she was doing, she bent suddenly and nuzzled her face against him. He groaned harshly and gripped her shoulders.

"Don't..."

She lifted her head slightly and looked up at him. "Giving up already?"

His mouth tightened. He shook his head and dropped his hands to his sides. The purpose of the contest was all but forgotten. It was a struggle now within himself and, too, in the age-old drama be-

tween male and female. Pride had become an issue.
He was determined not to give in.

Unless, of course, he could do it on his own terms.

"Not bad," he murmured, then deliberately added,
"for an amateur."

She stepped back slightly and straightened. Her
hands were on her hips, so that the tacky old plaid
shirt was pulled snugly over her breasts. Her eyes
looked smoke-filled.

"You'd prefer a professional?"

He chuckled. "I never have and I don't plan to start
now."

"I'm so glad to hear that. By the way, besides those
beautiful eyes and this really extraordinary chest, you
have a very nice laugh. I wouldn't mind hearing it
more."

"Keep on the way you're going and you're sure to."
At her quizzical look, he explained, "I'm ticklish."

She smiled broadly. "You'd put a piece of information like that in the hands of a gambling woman?"

"Obviously you're not aware of the theory that
tickling suppresses the libido."

"No," she agreed, "I'm not. Still, no sense taking
chances. You be sure to tell me if you feel even the
slightest bit of tickling. For instance, does this...?"
With one finger, she scratched a feather-light line
down his chest following the dark thatch of hair.
Slowly, she dipped the finger beneath his waistband
and circled the indentation of his naval.

"Feel anything?" she asked, her eyes wide with
devilment.

"Not a thing," he assured her gravely.

"That's good," she whispered, breath light on the
thick column of his neck, "because I'd hate to stop."

Yet she might have to soon because she was feeling more than a little light-headed. Her breasts were full and swollen, the nipples acutely sensitive against the thin lace of her bra. There was a damp, hot tightening between her thighs and a flutter in her stomach that grew stronger by the moment.

No doubt about it, girl, she told herself, you're in over your head and sinking fast. But she couldn't let that stop her, not when she could feel the heat and power of him so very close. He stood absolutely still but she felt the tremors racing through him and was emboldened by them.

Had the circumstances been different, she would never have been so daring. But his concern about hurting her and her determination to make him realize that he could still trust himself combined to throw off all restraint.

She took a deep, shuddering breath and undid the button of his waistband. As she did so, her hand brushed his erection. He made a harsh, grating sound and closed his fingers around her wrist.

This time she knew better than to taunt him. His eyes were narrowed to razor points of light. A dull flush of color darkened his cheeks. His mouth was firmly drawn and as she watched, his chest rose and fell swiftly.

"Lady," he murmured, "you're playing with fire."

Her tongue touched her lips nervously. "I'm not playing at all."

He looked at her long and hard, feeling the rush of her pulse beneath his fingers. Slowly, he raised her hand to his mouth. His tongue touched the delicate underside of her wrist, tracing the blue web of her life's blood. He breathed in deeply, fighting the waves of desire that struck one after the other.

"My brother will never know what you've done for him," he said and took her mouth with his.

Chapter 14

Very deliberately, as though he were standing apart from himself watching every move he made, James took hold of the ugly plaid shirt and pulled it until the buttons gave one after another, falling onto the floor. All the while, he kept his eyes locked on Kristina's. If she was going to run, it would be now.

She stood absolutely still and let him do as he chose. Her eyes held no fear or hesitation, only complete trust and a desire so great that it made him feel humble.

"Let's get rid of this," he said huskily and pushed the shirt off her shoulders. It fell away, leaving her bare from the waist up except for a lacy scrap of cloth that concealed little. Her breasts were exquisite, high and firm, perfectly fitted to his hand, or his mouth. The nipples and surrounding areolae were large, rosy pink in color and swollen.

He breathed in deeply and put his hands around her waist. Slowly, he lifted her, moving her against him so that she could feel every inch of his arousal.

Shakily, she said, "I always thought the British were supposed to be very reserved."

His eyes flared. "Really?"

"In fact, everyone thinks that."

"You don't think this is proper British behavior?" he asked and touched his tongue to the fragrant cleft between her breasts.

She gasped as her head fell back.

"Or this?" he asked thickly. His teeth raked the delicate skin of her throat before closing lightly around her earlobe. Only his muscular arm around her waist kept her from falling.

She hardly knew when he lowered her onto the soft carpet in front of the fire. For a moment, he stood above her, powerful, indomitable. She lay, one leg bent, an arm folded beneath her head, and watched him with unabashed fascination as he stripped off the shirt she had undone. When he came down over her, covering her with his body, she welcomed him with unfeigned joy.

"I meant it," he whispered against the curve of her cheek, "I don't want to hurt you. You're so beautiful, so sweet . . . perfect."

"I want you so much," she murmured and realized with a start that it was completely true. In fact, wanting didn't really describe it. She hungered for this man, needing him in a way she had never known before. She, who had always prided herself on being self-sufficient, felt starkly incomplete without him.

She raised her arms, closing them around his broad, sinewy back. He felt so big and powerful, yet he trembled against her. She moved slightly, her cleft brushing against his erection. A soft gasp broke from her.

He raised himself on his arms and smiled. "Still feel like gambling?"

By way of an answer, she drew his head back down to hers. His kiss was commanding. He explored her mouth with careful thoroughness, not thrusting too aggressively but drawing her irresistibly into the rhythm of his movements. Their limbs entwined, bodies searching, hands and lips discovering.

Her bra closed in the front. He unhooked it deftly and slipped it off. Carefully, he cupped her breasts in his palms, his thumbs rubbing over the turgid nipples.

"So sweet," he murmured as he bent his head, catching first one erect crest in his mouth and then the other. He suckled her gently but so powerfully that she felt a tugging deep within her womb and moaned.

Her hands tangled in his hair, holding him close. Long, exquisite moments passed before she could bear it no longer. Her back arched and her legs fell apart.

He raised his head, staring down at her. Softly, he said, "You're sure..."

"Oh, God, yes. Please..."

No further encouragement was needed. Quickly, he rose and stripped off his remaining clothes. Her breath caught as she stared at him. Naked, he was magnificent, broad-chested, long-limbed, more then amply endowed. Her throat tightened as she stared at his manhood surrounded by the thick thatch of dark hair. She wanted him so desperately, needed him, but faint uncertainty stirred in her.

He saw it and moved quickly to reassure her. With exquisite gentleness, he slipped her jeans off, his lips and tongue laving her flat tummy. Slowly, he parted her thighs further, his fingers stroking the sensitive inner skin. All the while he murmured encouragement.

"So lovely, sweet and hot . . . so welcoming . . ."

She twisted under him, gasping his name. His hand slid farther between her legs, stroking the sensitive nub of flesh hidden there. Heat suffused her. The firelight was dancing. She smelled fragrant smoke, dried herbs, the promise of spring, all mingling with the musky scent of their bodies cleaving to one another.

The tip of his manhood touched her lightly. He bent, kissing her again and again even as he began slowly and smoothly to enter her.

She stood it as long as she could until the pleasure became too much and she surged against him. He cried out her name and went very still, holding himself deep within her until she had time to adjust to his fullness.

Only then did he begin to move again, drawing her with him into hot, surging pleasure that grew with each powerful thrust until at last the long, throbbing release seized them both.

When Kristina awoke, she was lying on her side, facing the fire. Beneath a silk coverlet, her body was bare. She stretched languidly and sat up slightly to look around. Before she got very far, her back bumped into something very hard, very warm and very close.

James.

"Hi, there," he said. The smile he gave her was pure satisfied male but his eyes were tender.

"Hi, yourself," she whispered and found she had difficulty forming the words. Little things like speech seemed to have gotten beyond her.

Sweet heaven, she had never felt anything like this, never even guessed that it was possible. No wonder he'd been instinctively cautious. This kind of thing could rock worlds.

His brows drew together as he saw her preoccupation. Softly, he asked, "Are you all right?"

No, of course she wasn't. For one thing, she didn't even feel like herself. But he didn't mean that, he meant the tenderness between her thighs. It was mild, to say the least, when compared to the exquisite pleasure she had experienced. Without a twinge of guilt for the small lie she was about to tell, she nodded.

"I'm fine. You?"

He laughed and lay back with his head pillowed on his arm. She snuggled close against him, listening to the beat of his heart. "Relieved, I suppose," he said. "I was really worried about hurting you."

"And now you can stop worrying," she said.

"About that."

"There's something else?" Belatedly, she remembered the bet and wondered if he was concerned about meeting the terms. But instead, he said, "You keep telling me I have to accept that I've changed. If this was anything to go by, I don't have much choice."

She breathed a silent prayer of thanks that he had come so far and touched her fingers to his mouth gently. "I don't know what you used to be like James

Wyndham, but I know what you're like now. You've nothing to regret."

He didn't answer at once, his gaze turned inward to some landscape she could not glimpse. But she sensed that he was thinking about his brother again. Finally, he shrugged and said, "We'll see."

He turned over, drawing her beneath him. His hand slipped beneath the silk to find and cup her breast. "It's raining again," he murmured. "Any chance I can persuade you to spend the night?"

"Some," she murmured. "A little more . . . mmm . . . I'd say the odds are turning in your favor."

"I love the sounds you make," he said against her throat. "The way you taste, the feel of you . . ."

He pushed the coverlet aside and bent over her, savoring the beautiful woman stretched out beneath him with an undeniable possessiveness. As his hands and mouth began to caress her, her eyes drifted shut.

It was on the tip of her tongue to say that she, too, loved and what she loved, but she stopped herself. She was too well aware that she had seduced him into an intimacy that he had tried to resist. He was a proud man and a private one who was still healing from a harrowing experience.

Later, she told herself, there would be time.

"We're going to give a party," Kristina announced. She looked at the startled faces of her students and grinned. "You heard me. We've just about finished restoring the castle to the way it was in the thirteenth century and we're going to celebrate. Any suggestions?"

"We all hit the nearest McDonald's?" one of the young women students suggested hopefully.

"We take part of the grant and head for the south of France," another ventured. Quickly, he added, "To study medieval trading contracts with Britain, of course."

"That's the problem with the younger generation," Kristina said, ignoring the fact that she was only a few years older than her students, "no imagination. What I have in mind, children, is a banquet. The real thing, if you please, with all the locals invited to sup within the walls of Innishffarin just as they would have in days gone by."

One by one, the students looked at each other. Was she serious? A medieval banquet complete with all the trimmings? Yes, apparently she was. Maybe they shouldn't be surprised. Recently, sane, sensible Professor McGinnis had been revealing an unexpectedly frolicsome side of her nature.

"Okay," Frank Standish said slowly, "that sounds good, but to do it up right will take work."

This brought groans all around but they broke off as Kristina raised her hand. "Not to worry. The staff over at Wyndham Manor has kindly agreed to help."

Eyebrows rose in unison and a few knowing smiles flashed. It hadn't escaped her students' notice that Professor McGinnis had spent several nights at the manor. They presumed she had a good reason—one named James Wyndham. The women envied her and the men were philosophical. He was, after all, the laird.

"That's nice of them," Frank said. "When are we going to do this?"

"Next Saturday," Kristina told him and laughed at the startled exclamations. "The whole village is invited, along with any tourists who happen to be in the area and everyone from the manor."

She didn't add that she hoped Richard Wyndham would also attend, but she thought it. In the days since her audacious wager with James, he had said nothing about his brother. She didn't ask when he intended to speak to him but neither did she doubt that he would. As difficult as he might find it, he would do what was right.

Of course, that didn't mean that he couldn't be helped a little.

Later that afternoon, when she stopped by the village to pick up a few supplies and begin spreading the word about the banquet, she dropped a note in the mail. It was addressed to Richard and it said simply that there was to be a party at the castle and he would be welcome.

Barely had the letter disappeared into the red Royal Mail box than she was seized by doubts about what she had done. She might well be going too far in involving herself with the brothers' problems. But it was too late now. She had to trust her instincts that it would all work out for the best.

Meanwhile, there was far too much to do to worry about anything else.

She began by planning the menu. Since those popular medieval standbys, boar and swan, were not readily available, a little creative license was called for. To begin with, she thought it wise to consult with Mary Horliss, grocer *extraordinaire* and not incidentally, the best source of information in all of Innishffarin.

"A party, you say?" the plump, motherly woman exclaimed. So great was her excitement that she actually hoisted herself up on her stool, slapped her hand against the counter and chortled. "Just what this old place needs, if you ask me. Splendid idea."

"I'm glad you approve," Kristina said solemnly. "However, I should warn you, we need help."

"And when have the villagers not helped prepare for a grand do at the Castle? Why, I remember the stories my mother used to tell me and her mother as well, the great fetes and tourneys, the banquets and market days. The villagers were always in the thick of things back then."

"Back when?" Kristina asked bemusedly. The castle had been far from a ruin when she and her students arrived but neither had it been lived in for some time. When in living memory would the villagers have flocked there for celebrations?

"Oh, centuries ago," Mrs. Horliss said, waving a hand dismissively at the notion that all that much time mattered. "My grandmother had the stories from her mother and she from hers. Many a time I used to sit on her lap listening to tales of how it used to be. Why kings came here, you know, Black Richard for one, although I always thought he deserved a better reputation than he ended up with. Several of the Henrys visited, there were so many of them I can never keep them straight. And then, of course, the Bonnie Prince spent a night or two."

"He seems to have spent a night or two everywhere in Scotland," Kristina said skeptically. In her opinion, tales of the ill-fated Bonnie Prince Charlie were too common to be trusted.

"Ah, now that's the truth," Mrs. Horliss admitted. "Fact is, I'm not sure about him coming. No one here could remember seeing him whereas they could remember the others clear enough. Of course," she added, "he could have come at night, being on the run and all."

"I'm sure," Kristina murmured.

"Never mind about him now. What sort of party did you have in mind?"

Kristina grinned. "A thirteenth-century one, to celebrate the restoration of the castle to the way it was back then."

Mrs. Horliss's eyes widened. "That's no easy thing you're speaking of."

"I know. To begin with, there's the food."

She got no further. Mrs. Horliss had gotten off her stool and was heading toward the back of the shop.

"Come with me," she said over her shoulder. "My grannie left me something you might want to take a look at."

The something was a book of recipes that had been written down, not by Mrs. Horliss's grannie who only inherited the book, but by her own great-grandmother writing in the seventeenth century. That long ago—Lady Winifred by name—had included a fine selection of family favorites, many which she noted were "in the olden ways."

They were indeed, Kristina thought happily. Best yet, Winifred had taken pains to explain everything in detail. She noted the proper techniques for "braying" and "seething," how to make almond milk and verjuice, and even how to prepare the essential manchet bread that was used instead of plates. Although Kristina thought that in this case she would forego kneading the dough with her feet as recommended, the book was definitely a find.

"May I borrow this?" she asked.

Mrs. Horliss nodded. "Sure you can. As soon as you've decided on the menu, let me know and I'll put the word out. How many people are you expecting?"

"I don't really know," Kristina admitted. "However many want to come, I suppose."

"Better plan on several hundred then," Mrs. Horliss said matter-of-factly. Her smile was broad. "In the old days, we brought food up to the castle by the wagon load. It sounds as though we'll be doing it again."

Bernard Berkowitz agreed. When Kristina met with him at the castle a short time later, he studied the book she had gotten from Mrs. Horliss, looked around at the bustle of activity already underway in the bailey, and said, "This is quite an undertaking, miss. However, rest assured that the staff will provide all possible help."

True to his word, he rolled up his sleeves and promptly got to work, along with half a dozen young footmen and stable hands he had brought along for, as he said, "the experience."

"How are you at making verjuice?" Kristina asked him later in the day as she passed by where he and the others were nailing together long trestle tables.

He thought for a moment, his brow mildly furrowed. "The juice of various unripe fruits mixed with rose hips? I believe I can manage that."

Kristina repressed a sigh. She refused to ask how a twentieth-century butler had at his fingertips the rec-

ipe for a medieval kitchen staple. Better to just leave
him to it.

Besides, she had other things to concern herself
with. James had sent over a spice chest, brought from
the East by some long-distant Wyndham ancestor. It
was the size of a small trunk and exquisitely made of
incised wood and hand-tooled leather. Instead of a lid
on the top, it opened from the front to reveal dozens
of tiny drawers each holding a different treasure—
thin, twisting strands of saffron, tiny beads of black
pepper, ground cumin, coriander, ginger, cardamom,
cloves, cinnamon, aniseed and even grains of rare pa-
prika.

Kristina thought of the generations of Wyndham
chatelaines who had daily parceled out the spices from
each drawer, guarding them for the rare and precious
things they were. She thought, too, of the Wyndham
men who had gone out in great ships—first the beak-
prowed Viking boats and the brave leather curraghs
and then later the high-masted sailing vessels that had
spanned the world. So much struggle and daring, adventure and, on occasion, tragedy.

She shook her head to clear it and closed the lid of
the chest firmly. The mingled perfumes of the spices
made her senses swim. For a moment, she seemed almost to see the swirling pennants and prancing horses,
hear the clang of steel and the shouts of men, feel in
her very skin the echo of passions long gone yet still
reverberating within the castle's ancient stone walls.

It was an illusion, of course, born of a certain over-
excitement and fatigue. Her life had taken a strange
and unexpected turn when she met James Wyndham.
He shattered her preoccupation with the past and

made her think far more about the future than she had ever done before.

But uncertainty lay in that direction. She shied from it, telling herself to take one day at a time and not ask for more than she had already been given.

And truly, she was trying to do just that—even managing it—when strong hands closed around her waist, a warm breath of laughter touched her cheek and she turned to find him smiling at her.

Chapter 15

"Come away," he said and took her hand in his.

She went, for truly how could she not? The preparations were well underway, she told herself. There was ample help. She would not be missed and indeed, no one gave them so much as a glance as they walked down the path to the beach where he had left the gray stallion.

Together, they rode along the shore until they came again to the ancient stone ruin and beyond it the hidden pool. Kristina thought suddenly of seeing him there and flushed. It seemed an age ago yet no more time than a breath had passed.

Yet everything had changed.

The day was unusually warm. Sunlight beat down on them as they walked hand in hand up from the beach. They spoke little, content with silence, until they reached the pool's edge. James paused, his eyes gentle on her.

"You've been working too hard," he said.

She shook her head. "Not so." If she looked tired, it was because she was getting so little sleep and who did he suppose was to blame for that?

"Bernie says you've worked wonders."

Pleased, for she admired and liked the butler, she asked, "Did he really? He's exaggerating. Everyone's done wonders. Without so much help, we wouldn't be anywhere near so far along."

"I'm glad you thought of the party," he said as he crouched down beside the pool and dipped a hand into the water. "You've brought life back to Innishffarin. It ought to be celebrated."

"There's another reason, too," she said as she knelt down beside him. "You ought to know it."

He looked at her quizzically. "What's that?"

"The villagers, the people at the manor, everyone wants to celebrate the laird's homecoming. I just gave them a handy way to do it."

She knew she was right about that. The outpouring of enthusiasm from the villagers and everyone else had been overwhelming. They would never have extended themselves so far merely for their own sakes. It was James they were thinking of, and his safe return for which they prepared to give thanks.

To her, that seemed only right but he actually appeared surprised. "I hadn't thought of that," he admitted and looked uncertain, as though he had mixed feelings about being at the center of such attention.

"Then don't," she said with a smile. "It's just something they want to do. Nobody expects you to take any part, except show up, of course."

"Oh, I'll do that, all right," he assured her. He turned, his eyes drifting over her in a way that was at once audacious and delightful. "In fact," he added softly, "I wouldn't miss it for the world."

The light touch of laughter in his voice warmed her. In the past few days, they had laughed much and loved often. Despite all the work she had to do, and his own vast responsibilities, they had found stolen hours to be together just as they were doing now.

Softly, she reached out and touched his face, tracing the square line of his jaw with her fingertip. He looked far more relaxed than he had before. The lines around his mouth were eased and there were fewer shadows in the crystalline blue eyes. She could almost see how he had looked as a boy, before the weight of duty and power began to take its toll.

She reached down, dappling the water with her fingers. "It's almost warm."

"You haven't been in it."

"No, but you were the other day and you survived."

"I kept some of my clothes on," he pointed out, a smile tugging at the corners of his mouth.

"We could try that."

"Of course, it is much warmer today. Practically hot."

"I wouldn't go that far," she said with a laugh.

His smile deepened. "Exactly how far would you go, Professor McGinnis?"

To the stars and back, she thought, for this man, but she didn't say so. The moment was too fragile.

Instead, she merely raised her hands to the length of ribbon holding her hair, pulled it free and said, "Let's see, shall we?"

He touched her with slow, consummate tenderness, removing her garments one by one. They took turns helping each other undress until a pile of clothing lay on the ground at their feet.

When she stood naked in front of him, his eyes raked over her, taking in the high-pointed breasts darkened at the tips by rosy areolae already hardening with desire, the slim curve of her waist and the ripeness of her hips. Her thighs were long and slender, parted in the center by a cluster of soft curls as sun-kissed as the hair on her head.

His throat tightened. He had to clench his hands into fists to keep from reaching for her right then. The need to go slow and savor the moment warred with the driving urge to lay her down on the moss-covered ground and possess her immediately.

Restraint won out, but only barely.

Kristina bore his scrutiny with pride. She knew he found her desirable and relished the growing confidence he inspired in her own womanhood. It took only a glance at the lambent flames flaring in his eyes, the faint tremor of his lean, powerful body to realize the extent of his need for her. When she let her eyes drift lower, to his erect manhood, her breath caught.

He was so beautiful, the epitome of masculine strength and power, broad of chest and shoulder, long-limbed, each muscle and sinew perfectly formed beneath burnished skin. So different from herself and yet the perfect complement to her own strength—and need.

Her hand reached out to him. Daringly, she stroked down his hair-roughened chest, over his flat belly, to cup him lightly. Her fingers closed carefully, caressing the length of him as her breath quickened.

He gave a low, husky groan and closed his hand over hers to stop her. "I can't take much of that," he said with a faint, disparaging laugh, "and I want this to last."

So did she, Kristina realized. She wanted to spin out this enchanted interlude as long as she possibly could manage it. Time, always her ally and her friend, was suddenly the enemy. If she could have stopped it, she would have, yet she could not have said why. She knew only that she was suddenly, almost terrifyingly afraid.

The sensation passed almost as swiftly as it came. Nothing had changed around them. The sylvan pool was the same, their privacy remained complete, yet she felt as though she had received a warning of darker times to come. Rather than consider it, she took a quick step forward so that her body brushed against the heated length of his own.

"So beautiful," James murmured deep in his throat. His big hands, the palms slightly callused from long hours in the saddle, cupped her swollen breasts. Skilled fingers teased her aching nipples as his mouth claimed her. Helpless to deny him anything, her lips parted for his probing tongue. He tasted her sweetness as his hands stroked down the long length of her back to lightly squeeze her buttocks.

A low, anguished groan broke from her. Abruptly, he knelt, blazing a line of fire kisses from her ripe breasts down the silken smoothness of her hips and belly. Shuddering uncontrollably, she whimpered his name. Mingled dismay and delight tore through her as his fingers separated the damp cleft of her womanhood. His tongue moved slowly, lingeringly over the ultrasensitive bud within. She cried out and gripped his shoulders as her knees gave way.

He rose in a quick, fluid motion and eased her gently to the ground. Swiftly, he covered her body with his own. Her hips arched invitingly, her eyes implored him, but still he held back.

Ignoring her whimpers of pleasure, he turned her over, positioning her between his thighs and began slowly but deliberately to caress her. His long, powerful fingers massaged the muscles of her shoulders and back, moving gradually downward to her thighs, the calves of her legs, her feet. Every inch of her knew his touch except where she desired it most. Her head tossed from side to side against the fragrant earth. When she tried almost desperately to turn over, he stopped her.

"Not yet," he growled deep in his throat. Speech was almost beyond him, so consuming was his need. But beyond it, overriding all else, was the need to give her the greatest possible pleasure. Deliberately, he drew out her arousal. His hands closed again around her taut derriere, kneading lightly even as his knee pushed between her legs, parting them.

Slowly, he slipped a long finger between the silken folds. At the same time, he wrapped an arm around her waist and lifted her slightly. Her hands clenched against the ground. Low, whimpering sounds broke the silence around them. His breath rasped in his chest. He spread her legs still farther apart and positioning her, thrust deep within.

She rocked back against him, taking him yet deeper. For several moments, he remained unmoving, his teeth clenched against the undulating waves of pleasure that engulfed him. When he thrust at last, he did so deeply and surely, and was rewarded by the spasms of her body as she found release.

He followed swiftly, gasping her name. Together, they collapsed back onto the ground, still intimately entwined.

"You can die from this," Kristina said a long time later when she could speak again.

"Maybe so," James agreed. He lay on his back, his eyes closed. His breathing was regular again and his heartbeat had returned to normal. He looked, she thought, like a magnificent animal whose needs had all been satisfied and who now lay replete and content.

"You don't sound very concerned," she said, her fingers curling in the thick nest of hair on his chest. When he didn't answer, she tugged lightly.

He opened one eye and scowled at her. "You're very daring."

"Oh, no, not me," she assured him. "Not daring at all. After all, what can you do? You just wore yourself out."

The other eye opened. "Did I?"

"Of course. Everyone knows women have far more stamina than men, especially in the...mmm...libido department."

"Everyone knows that, do they?"

"Indubitably, but I'd never be one to rub it in. You have a nice rest. I'm going for a swim."

She got up just in time to avoid his quick lunge. He fell back, muttering about the nerviness of women. Laughing, she ran to the pool and dived in, cutting the water cleanly. The first touch was invigorating, the next numbing. She came up sputtering.

"Nice and warm, is it?" he drawled.

"Just fine," she lied. Actually, she was getting used to it quickly enough. The pool was in direct sunlight and undoubtedly far more comfortable than the nearby sea. After she paddled around a little, it didn't feel bad at all.

She swam leisurely back and forth, enjoying the cool silken feel of the water and the warmth of the sun on her back. Lazily, she turned over and let herself float, drifting into the shallower water on the far side of the pool.

Clouds moved gracefully above her. She smelled the perfume of heather and sea grass mingling with a freshening breeze. The day was perfect, made all the more so by the knowledge that James was nearby.

Indeed, nearer than she realized. He had entered the water so smoothly and quietly that he was almost next to her before she heard him. Only when she felt his hand close around her ankle did she open her eyes with at start, just in time to see him grinning at her.

"Breathe!" he ordered, gave her a moment to do so, and then pulled them both underwater.

The pond was almost crystal clear. Beneath the surface, the rock walls shone whitely. Tendrils of drifting grasses rose from the bottom. It was exquisitely beautiful, a place of enchantment. They rose again, showering water droplets in all directions and breathed deeply.

"Incredible," she murmured, looking at him. His skin glowed as the powerful muscles of his shoulders and back flexed. In the shallows where he stood, the water reached no higher than his hips. He threw back his head, tossing the hair from his eyes, and let his gaze move over her.

"Delightful," he agreed.

"There aren't supposed to be any places left like this," she said, "and certainly none in the wilds of Scotland."

"Perhaps it's a faerie gift," he suggested, straight-faced.

"Do you really think so?" she asked, matching his seriousness.

"I don't see why not. There have always been tales of faerie doings in these parts. Ireland's not the only place with its little people."

"You're teasing," she accused, thinking wistfully of how nice the world would be if magic truly did exist.

"Am I?" he asked. "There's a time I would have been but lately..." He broke off as she came nearer. Slowly, their bodies touched.

"Lately," he went on as her arms went around his neck, "I've begun to think anything's possible."

Kristina couldn't have agreed with him more. The limitations of the real world no longer seemed to exist. They drifted together, paddling slowly through the silken waters, until a cloud drifted over the sun. When she shivered, he drew her closer and lifted her from the water.

"I suppose we should get back," he said.

Reluctantly, she agreed. They dressed slowly, delaying as long as they could. The gray stallion carried them both back down the beach. The castle walls rose above them as James said, "I have to go to New York for a few days but I'll be back by the weekend."

She nodded against his chest, knowing she would miss him terribly but also relieved almost that she would have a little time in which to sort through her feelings. She needed to take a step back, to reestablish some semblance of control over herself.

Yet even as she decided that, she realized that it was a foolish goal. With James there was no going back. Like it or not, the future rushed at them.

Chapter 16

By Thursday—two days before the party—Kristina felt that she could take a deep breath and start to believe they really would be ready on time. Once taken with the idea, her students had outdone themselves stitching costumes, arranging entertainment, setting up displays about medieval life, and generally throwing themselves into the swim.

At the same time—with the help of the manor servants led by Bernie and the indomitable Mrs. Horliss—Kristina had prepared enough food to feed a medieval army, which she had on good authority, was what was about to descend on her.

"Everyone's coming," Mrs. Horliss said with palpable satisfaction. "I talked to my sister in Glasgow. She said she wouldn't miss it for the world. Bringing her four children she is, and two grandkids to boot. And that's just for starters. The whole village's been on the phone. It's amazing to me the wires don't overheat. Every niece and nephew, cousin and in-law has said they'll be here."

She looked critically at the mass of small golden pies on the trestle table in front of them and said, "Best make a few dozen more pasties, don't you think?"

"We've made hundreds," Kristina said with a soft groan but she reached for a sack of flour even as she spoke.

"Pasties always are popular," Mrs. Horliss said as she hitched her sleeves up again. "Them and the apple tarts'll go fast, count on it."

"Mr. Berkowitz said he'd take care of the eels," Kristina said gratefully. She'd never been squeamish but the idea of coping with barrelfuls of squirming conger eels which had to be among the ugliest and angriest looking things she had ever seen was beyond her.

"Can't have a proper do without eel," Mrs. Horliss agreed. "Not without haggis, either, if you ask me."

"Haggis isn't in the cookbook," Kristina pointed out. She couldn't imagine how it had been overlooked, being the national dish of Scotland, but she was grateful all the same.

The one time she'd come face to face with a dish of sheep's entrails cooked in the stomach, she'd realized straightaway why it was always accompanied by large measures of whiskey. Nothing less could have made it palatable.

"Besides," she added, "we've got plenty without it. The food booths will be set up in the bailey. People can walk around and help themselves. The pub's sending up the casks of beer and cider tomorrow. The tables are already in place. Everything's going to be fine."

"Aye," Mrs. Horliss said softly and patted Kristina's cheek lightly, leaving a smudge of flour along it. "It's a splendid thing you've done, getting everyone together this way. Now if only Mr. Richard comes..."

Kristina didn't comment but privately she wondered if he would. There had been no reply to her note. She didn't even know for certain that he had gotten it.

And anyway, perhaps if he didn't come it would be for the best. The parallels between this party and the one given so long ago to celebrate another Wyndham son's return were beginning to disturb her.

She'd given them no thought at first, but now she kept remembering all the details of the event Linus had so carefully recorded. With a start, she realized that they were even serving some of the same dishes that had been presented at that long-ago banquet. As there had been on that day, mimes, singers and minstrels would stroll around the bailey, booths would be set up and pennants would fly.

There would be great joy but also lingering questions and a breach between brothers that still showed no sign of healing.

She shook her head ruefully. Her imagination was running away with her. Probably the result of making too many pasties, she decided. The past did not repeat itself. She had to remember that.

But it still did hold fascinating secrets and it was of them that she thought when she finally finished in the kitchens and went back into the courtyard for some fresh air.

It was late afternoon. The busy activity of the day was beginning to die down. Many of the villagers had gone home and her students were taking their ease before beginning preparations for supper. She had a few hours to herself, the first few since returning from London.

Once again she thought of Linus and the detailed description he had left of that day so long ago. And of what had caused the bitter falling out between the brothers.

All thought of scaling the cliff side had been put firmly out of her head. If she was going to find any clue to the mysterious sea cliff where the cross had been found, it would have to be from inside the castle. Although she expected very little success, she decided to explore further.

As always, she found herself in the back corridor of the castle. That made sense in a way, for it was the side that faced outward in the direction of the sea. But it also yielded nothing.

The corridor stretched about two hundred feet, ending at a small wooden door that she already knew led outside the castle. Iron brackets were set in the wall at regular intervals. Long ago they had held torches dipped in pitch and tar whose flames had blackened the ceiling above.

More recently, they had been empty. Now once again the torches were in place, for the sake of authenticity, but they remained unlit.

The granite blocks that formed the walls were large and smoothly cut. The ceiling was low enough that she could reach even the topmost ones by simply standing on tiptoe.

It had occurred to her early on that one of the stones—or possibly more than one—might conceal the entrance to a hidden passage. Certainly the walls were thick enough to contain such a thing. But try as she might, she could not budge a single stone. Despite their great age, they all remained firmly in place.

The floor was another matter. Here the passage of the years had caused the stones to sink slightly, more so in the middle where people tended to walk than on either side. It was possible that a secret entrance could be located in the floor but again, despite her best efforts, she could find no sign of it.

James had said that the passage was sealed up after the cross was found. With that to inspire her, she searched diligently for any sign of recent work, recent being in the last couple of centuries.

There were none. To a remarkable degree, Innishffarin stood just as it always had done, almost untouched by the passage of time.

Long ago, another young woman—Katlin Sinclair by name—had come down this passage. Kristina didn't know for certain what had led her to search so diligently for the Wyndham treasure but she alone of all the generations who had looked had been successful. It was Katlin who found the cross and who shortly thereafter became Katlin Wyndham.

Kristina tried to imagine what she had felt as she searched. Had she had better information, some clue that led her on? Or had she depended on her own intelligence and perseverance?

One side of the passage was the outer wall, on the other was a series of small rooms that had been used for storage in the past, except for one which, as Kristina recalled, had been a chapel. On impulse, she opened the door to it only to stop where she was.

Darkness obscured the small chamber. Lacking a torch, she could see little. Worse yet, she could hear off in the distance the bell ringing to call everyone to supper. She had been longer in the back passage than she'd realized. Night was falling fast.

Frustration gripped her. She was almost willing to believe that the Wyndham clan was right—no treasure remained to be found. But Linus had been so precise in his description and, so far, he'd not been wrong about anything else.

Besides, if there had been a ghostly guardian, he had come from a much later time. Perhaps he'd been no better informed than the rest of the family.

That she was seriously entertaining such a notion made her shake her head in annoyance. The bell rang again. Right on cue, her stomach growled, reminding her that though she had spent the day cooking, she'd had almost nothing to eat.

Before she could think any more about it, she shut the door again and turned to go, but not without promising herself that she'd return as soon as she could for another look.

He came to her in the night, stepping into the small chamber where she slept as soundlessly as the moon slipped through the sky. For a time, he was content to merely stand and look at her, asleep on the narrow cot. Her hair was neatly braided and tied with bright ribbons. She wore a thin shift that had slipped off her shoulder, exposing the curve of skin glowing alabaster in the faint light.

James took a deep breath and let it out slowly. He was very tired, having worked straight through the days in New York so that he could take the earliest possible flight back. Even then he had stayed awake, plowing through yet more work as the sleek jet sped across the sky.

Then had come the swift ride from the airport—too swift, he supposed he had broken a few speeding laws along the way. Even then he'd known he should get to the manor and get a least a few hours sleep. But Innishffarin and the woman within proved irresistible.

He put a hand to his tie and loosened it. She slept so peacefully, almost like a child. Yet this was no innocent before him but a woman with strength and passion who had breached the solitude of his nature and made herself indispensable to him in a way he would never have thought possible.

He would have to tell her that, he decided, before too much longer. But for the moment . . .

Soundlessly, he stripped off the trappings of the modern world, the pinstripe suit and handmade shirt, the fine leather shoes and even the paper thin and outrageously expensive watch he favored.

All these he placed neatly in a pile near the door. Only then did he step farther into the room.

Still, she did not move. Moonlight silvered the curve of her cheek and lay lovingly over the swell of her breasts. She had pushed the covers back. He could see the dark rose crests of her nipples and the delicate curve of her waist.

A slim hand lay folded near her cheek. He reached for it gently and touched his mouth to the delicate skin of her palm. She stirred and murmured softly.

Kristina woke from a dream of splashing sun and laughing water to find a dark shape above her bed. She blinked once, twice, and opened her arms.

"I should scream," she whispered as he came down onto the cot with her. "It'd be what you deserve. Barging in here in the middle of the night with no warning."

"Do you want to scream?" he asked languidly as he traced the delicate line of her cheek.

"Not particularly."

"Takes too much effort, right?"

"Exactly, which could be used for better things."

"Like what?" he asked.

"Oh, this..." She ran a hand down his chest and gave a little exclamation of surprise when she discovered he was completely naked. "And that..."

It was his turn to react, which he did most gratifyingly. Kristina laughed softly and turned to face him. Their noses bumped.

"Ouch," she said.

"Who's idea was this anyway?" he asked.

"I think we got this cot from a convent."

"There's always the floor," he suggested.

Her eyes widened as she thought of the hard stone that always managed to be cold no matter what the weather. "You wouldn't?"

"No," he relented, "I wouldn't. But where does that leave us?"

Kristina thought for a moment. Slowly, she smiled. "Come on," she said and stood up. "I've got a better idea."

It required that he put his clothes back on, at least some of them, and that she do the same, but in the end it proved worthwhile. Hand in hand, she led him up a staircase in the farthest tower, the one perched most defiantly toward the sea. At the top of the winding steps, a wooden doorway studded with iron gave way to a spacious chamber.

This room alone in all the castle the students had not touched, partly because it looked so lovely but also because it had been a condition of their use of the castle that they not do so. Kristina could not fault the urge to protect it.

Someone long ago had furnished it with a magnificent canopied bed hung with embroidered curtains, several charcoal braziers for warmth, a splendid Persian rug, and very little else.

Whatever the room had been used for, it wasn't for ordinary day-to-day living. On the contrary, it had all the earmarks of a place where lovers would go to be alone and undisturbed.

"I should have known you'd find this," James said with a low chuckle.

"I couldn't miss it. I've been over every inch of this castle but I have to admit, this room is my favorite."

"It belonged to Katlin and Angus Wyndham."

"I thought they lived at the manor?"

"They did but they..." He grinned devilishly. "Let's just say family legend has it all their children were conceived here."

A tremor ran through her. It was only a coincidence, but earlier in the day Kristina had been thinking about Katlin Sinclair, about how she was possibly following in Katlin's very footsteps, and here she was doing the same thing again. A soft smile touched her mouth. If the portrait she had seen in the manor was any indication, that long-ago Wyndham bride had been a woman of passion and courage.

Kristina felt certain Katlin would not mind that the secluded room she had designed for a lover's delight was still being used the same way.

James walked over to one of the windows set in the curve of the tower. He opened the heavy wooden shutters and beckoned to her. "Look."

She came to stand close against him. Together, they stared out over the sea. Moonlight spilled across the white-flecked water. The night was so clear and bright that it was possible to see far out toward the horizon. On such nights other lovers had stood where they stood now, watching the timeless flow of the sea and the stars.

Kristina sighed softly and tipped her head back against his broad shoulder. She had never felt more content in her life but that was not to last.

When his hands slipped beneath her loose shift to cup her breasts, urgency filled her. She turned in his arms and drew his mouth to hers.

Swiftly, they stripped away their clothes. The bed received them gently. James made a move above her but Kristina stopped him with a touch. Smiling, she pressed him onto his back.

''Let me,'' she murmured.

He acquiesced with such speed that she laughed. But the laughter died as the play turned serious. It was astounding, she thought, how this bold, proud man could tremble at her slightest touch.

She had only to trail a hand across the sculpted muscles of his torso to send a spasm down the length of his body. When she bent her leg slightly so that the silken smoothness of her inner thigh rubbed against his erection, he growled her name. Her lips pressed gently against his throat causing his hands to dig into the mattress.

A heady sense of power surged through her. Slowly, she moved over him, pausing to taste and caress until at last he could bear nothing more.

Big, callused hands grasped her hips and lifted her, holding her above him for a moment as their eyes met.

Gazes locked, he lowered her inch by inch onto him until he filled her completely. The piercing sense of being so totally possessed made her moan helplessly.

"Feel what you do to me," he commanded. The velvety inner walls of her body gave way before him, yielding to his demands. He stopped, tantalizingly, and lifted her again, up and down, up and down, all along the thick, hard shaft that pierced her so sweetly.

She cried out and dug her fingers into his shoulders. Deliberately, she rotated her hips in a way that made him cry out. He grasped her and turned quickly, positioning her under him. His powerful thighs opened her even wider. He withdrew completely and holding himself braced on his arms above her, looked down into her eyes.

"Take me into you."

Beyond speech, hardly able to breathe, she closed her hand around him and did as he said. He penetrated deeper and deeper, filling her so completely that she thought she could not possibly take more. His face taut, he waited until he was sure she had adjusted to him before he moved again, slowly and deeply.

With long, thorough thrusts, he came almost completely out of her before entering again and again. Her head tossed back and forth across the pillows. Her back arched, hips rising to draw him even deeper. She stopped, waiting, feeling what was coming, knowing it so well now, only a little more...

The release that seized her was shattering. She could only cling to him as his own climax swiftly followed. They lay together as the moonlight spilled through the open shutters, bathing the tower chamber in unearthly radiance.

Chapter 17

"Oyez, oyez," the herald called. "The gates of the castle being opened and at the order of the laird, all comers to be admitted, I do declare and proclaim this festival of Innishffarin to be begun! Good tidings all. Eat, drink—but not too much—and be merry! So his lordship wills!"

A great cheer went up from the several hundred villagers and visitors who gathered in the bailey yard. Standing with James on the steps leading to the great hall, Kristina looked out over the assemblage delightedly. She could hardly believe that so many had come or that they had so thrown themselves into the mood of the day. Almost every man, woman and child had contrived a costume of sorts, however vaguely medieval. There was Robin Hoods and harem girls, ladies with high conical hats and gentlemen dressed up as jesters. Everyone seemed set on a rip-roaring good time.

And why not? For as one after another shouted, they were there to welcome the laird home and they wanted him to know it.

James accepted their acclaim quietly. He did not shy from it, but stood dignified and courteous in a plain white shirt and dark pants, his hair brushed back from his high forehead, his expression slightly aloof. Only his eyes gave his feelings away. They were alight with pride and something perilously close to joy.

Kristina looked away hastily. She did not want to disgrace herself by exposing how much this meant to her, not here in front of so many people.

"All right, then," James said, "the party's begun. The pasty-eating contest starts in five minutes. I understand there are gentlemen here from Edinburgh who believe they can beat the lads of Innishffarin. Are they right?"

"No!" shouted the crowd and made as one toward the booth where the pasties were piled high. Mrs. Horliss stood there, arms folded beneath her ample bosom, looking barely different than she did on any day and yet somehow fitting in perfectly with the notion that the thirteenth century had somehow come back to life, if only for a few, fine hours.

"Stop that pushing," she ordered, "plenty for everyone. Contestants take your seats. Spectators over there out of the way. Hurry about now, the lot of you. We've plenty else to do."

Several dozen did as she said while others wandered off to explore. Kristina caught a glimpse of Frank showing a group of round-eyed children the game of pegs. Ben was nearby, holding a small boy's hand as he guided him through the intricacies of rolling a wooden hoop. Everywhere she looked, people were laughing and talking, gazing admiringly around the castle, and enjoying themselves thoroughly. Exactly as she had hoped.

Everyone, that was, except Richard. There was no sign of the younger Wyndham brother.

"They're waiting on you to crack the first barrel, your lordship," a young man said diffidently. By his scalp lock and the tattoo on his arm, Kristina guessed that he was more usually found at home on the back of a motorcycle. But on this day, when time rolled back, he was just another villager acknowledging the laird's bounty.

James stepped down off the steps and held out a hand to Kristina. Regretfully, she shook her head. "I've things to do. You go on."

He nodded, gave her a quick smile and went off, trailed by the young man. A moment later, she saw him in the middle of a group of men, laughing as the first fine froth of ale poured forth.

As for herself, she had promised Butler Berkowitz that she would help with the serving. She found him in the kitchens, supervising his ever-efficient if somewhat harried staff.

"Ah, there you are, miss," he said when he spotted her. "We're doing very well. The chicken and almond molds are done and the beef skewers will be ready momentarily."

She nodded, relieved to hear it. "That's a hungry crowd out there."

"So I gather," he said with a smile. "Innishffarin hasn't fed this many in several centuries. Careful with that," he added quickly as two young footmen stumbled past, carrying between them a cauldron of white bean soup.

"The breads are done," he continued when they were gone, "and the rolls are about to come out. We've still the ginger and bread puddings but it will be a while before they're needed."

"You've worked wonders," Kristina told him honestly. "No thirteenth-century butler could have done better."

He inclined his head gravely. "Thank you, miss. Butlering is an old and honorable profession. I don't mind reliving some of its glory days, if only briefly."

Satisfied that everything was under control in the kitchens, Kristina went back outside. A soft breeze was blowing off the sea. It flattened the simple white skirt she wore paired with a shirt of the same fabric. The shirt had puffed sleeves and over it she'd put on a laced bodice. She'd put the outfit together from clothes bought over the years at various out-of-the-way boutiques. Strictly speaking, there was nothing medieval about it. If anything, it was more late 1960s hippie. But it worked.

Her hair was done up in a single braid that hung down her back. She had bathed in lilac-scented water that morning and smelled of it still. The scent followed her as she crossed the crowded bailey, accepting the greetings of the people she passed, until she found James among the men.

Just as she did, Frank Standish saw them and promptly struck up a tune on his fiddle. "We're a little out of time with this instrument, folks, but I'm sure if they'd had it back then, they would have enjoyed it. What do you say to a good country reel?"

There was immediate acclamation for this and further demands that the laird should lead the dance. James made a halfhearted effort to refuse but gave in when he saw the light in Kristina's eyes. With a smile, he held out his hand.

"Professor?"

"We can drop the formalities for today," she told him as they walked side by side into the center of the bailey where an open spot was quickly cleared.

"Only for today?"

"Of course. I expect total respect at all other times."

"And isn't that what you've been getting?" he teased her.

"Oh, yes," she assured him. Solemnly, she added, "Deep, deep respect."

"Careful," he warned, his hand tightening on hers. "Don't start something you aren't prepared to finish."

"Who says I'm not?"

"Right here, in the bailey yard?"

Her cheeks flushed. He was playing with her but the light in his eyes suggested he would need very little encouragement to sweep her away. Back to the tower room, perhaps, or to the rock pond. Anywhere they could be alone together.

But first there was the day... and the dance.

Bow touched strings and music soared. The crowd took up the beat, clapping enthusiastically. James took a bow, she curtsied, and they stepped out together.

Years before, she had taken a folk-dancing course but had hardly used the skill since. She was surprised at how readily it came back to her. With James's strong arm around her waist, the world flew by.

She was vaguely aware of the crowd cheering them on and of others joining in, but nothing really mattered except the sheer joy she felt at being with him.

Too soon the music ended, but quickly enough another tune began. They danced until at last, breathless and laughing, she raised her hands in surrender.

"No, more," she pleaded. "I've got to sit this one out."

He agreed and took her arm, guiding her through the throng of well-wishers toward a quiet spot near the stable wall.

"How about some cold cider?" he asked when she was settled in the shade.

"Heavenly."

He went off to get it and returned a short time later with two chilled mugs. Kristina drained hers thirstily. James did the same. He wiped the back of his hand across his mouth and laughed. "Good lord, there's Mary Horliss kicking up her heels and the Right Reverend Goodbody with her. The Widow Corey's actually laughing and Wilburcross McDermott—who has not been known to crack a smile in well over fifty years—looks as though his face itself will crack if he smiles much more."

He turned to her and said gently, "Your party's a success, Kristina McGinnis. You've brought the light and the life back to this old place."

She flushed, warmed by his praise but touched also by how much he knew about his people.

"Not one of them is a stranger to you, are they? No matter how many other responsibilities you've had, you've kept up with everything here."

He looked surprised that she would even think that worth mentioning. "What else would I do? This is Innishffarin, after all, where everything began. London, New York, all the rest of it, is fine enough but nothing matters so much as this place and these people.''

"There aren't many who still feel that way," she said, thinking of how few ties most people seemed to have, almost as though they were afraid of them and thought that by avoiding or denying them they could make their lives easier, when all they succeeded in doing was making them meaningless.

Richard, for instance, who claimed that what he wanted more than anything else was simply a chance to talk with his brother. Yet who could not even come home to meet him.

Anger filled her at the injustice of that, and might have grown had James not been called just then to the archery contest. She went along to watch as he stood in the field beyond the castle, the bow rock-steady in his hands and shot the arrow true. Others tried as well, and a few came close, but it was his aim that carried the day.

The prize was a flagon of ale, which he was trying to persuade her to share, when they both became aware of a sudden ripple of silence moving through the crowd that moments before had been so boisterous.

She looked up then, toward the open gate of the castle, and saw in that instant what she had half-hoped and half-dreaded. Her anger at Richard was misplaced. He, too, had come home.

They sat down together at one of the trestle tables in the bailey. Richard was at his most cordial best. He teased his brother about the ease with which he had won the archery contest, complimented Kristina extravagantly on the fine job she'd done, and greeted all and sundry guests by name.

For their part, the villagers received him with mingled affection and caution. The smiles were ready enough but the glances that went from brother to brother were far more serious.

Kristina did her best to hide her apprehension as Richard joined them at the table. Slices of manchet bread were set at each place and individual goblets were available, both in a bow to modern tastes. Ordinarily, the bread would have been shared by two and goblets would have been passed among many.

The food was carried out on great trenchers borne aloft by two footmen each. In addition to the beef and chicken, the eels and the soup, there were eight other courses, making for a modest dozen in all. Twice that number would have been more in keeping with tradition but modern stomachs weren't up to it.

As delicious as everything was, Kristina ate little. She kept wondering what would happen when—and if—the brothers were alone. Richard did most of the talking, keeping up a running stream about events in London. He was very witty and made everyone who heard him laugh. Everyone, that is, except James, who sat quietly at the head of the table, his face unreadable.

Finally, when the desserts had been passed and everyone was replete, he leaned forward and said quietly, "I've tried to reach you."

Richard nodded but did not look at him. "I knew I was coming up. It seemed simpler to talk here."

"As you will," James said. He stood and stepped away from the table, waiting.

Richard had no choice. He cast a quick, shadowed glance at Kristina and followed him.

Chapter 18

Neither James nor Richard returned to the party. The afternoon waned and slowly the crowd—exhausted, disheveled and well satisfied—dispersed. Kristina helped to clean up but her mind was not on the work. When she dropped yet another plate, Bernie sent her packing.

"You've done your share and more," he told her. "Go and rest." Softly, he added, "Tomorrow is another day."

She gave him a grateful look but didn't trust herself to speak. Worry had brought tears too close to the surface.

Briefly, she thought of going for a walk on the beach but the sound of the waves which she had always enjoyed was suddenly mournful. The bright warmth of day was gone. In its place were chill shadows.

For a time, she tried working in her room. There were always notes to be made. But nothing could hold her attention. Finally, she gave up and stretched out on the cot.

Sleep would not come. She tossed and turned for half an hour before finally giving up. Gingerly, she rose, pulled on her clothes and flung a cape around her shoulders.

The bailey was deserted. The students were off to a well-deserved rest and everyone else had left. She crossed the open courtyard and went through the great hall. Slowly, she climbed the twisting staircase to the tower room.

With her hand on the iron latch of the door, she hesitated. Bittersweet memories of the hours she had spent there with James almost made her retreat. But she took a deep breath, pushed the door open and stepped inside.

The beauty of the room struck her immediately. Old as it was, it was in excellent repair. The shutters were closed against the night. She had only to strike a match to one of the braziers to make light dance against the ceiling and walls.

With a low sigh, she crawled into the bed, still wearing her white costume. She drew the cloak more tightly around her and shut her eyes, courting sleep.

She hadn't really expected it to happen but it was some unaccounted time later that she opened her eyes and realized she was not alone. The tower door, which she had shut behind her, stood open.

Kristina sat up in the bed. She leaned forward, hardly breathing. James cursed under his breath as the match he had used to find his way burned his fingers. He blew it out and came into the room.

"I thought you might be here," he said and sat down on the edge of the bed.

His shoulders slumped. He looked more exhausted than she had ever seen him. In an instant, she made a decision. All explanations—presuming he wanted to provide any—could wait. Just then he needed care.

Gently, she put her arms around him. He stiffened and for a moment she thought he would not accept the comfort she offered. But the weariness was too great, or perhaps the need. He laid his head on her shoulder and said quietly, "I'm glad I found you."

She nodded but said nothing, only moving over in the bed and drawing him with her. He paused only to pull his boots off before slipping under the covers. At first, he held her so tightly that she could hardly breathe. She could feel the tension in him, a terrible, unspoken anguish that made her throat tighten. But quickly, his grip eased as sleep took him.

Kristina remained awake. She lay with her arms around him, his head close to her breasts, safeguarding him as best she could through the long, dark night. Twice he cried out, once she thought it was Richard's name he spoke. But she soothed him with gentle murmurings as she might use with a child and he slipped away again into unconsciousness.

Yet never did he fully release his hold on her. Even when his breathing was deepest and most regular, he kept her close. Deep in the night, Kristina, too, fell away into sleep. When she woke again, a faint gray rim of light was visible over the sea, through the pair of open shutters.

James stood before them, his back to her. He seemed completely absorbed in his thoughts yet he heard her the moment she stirred and turned back to the room.

He was fully dressed even to his boots. His shoulders were straight, his head high. He looked very little like the ravaged man who had come to her the night before, except in the eyes where deep, pain-filled shadows lingered.

"I have to go," he said.

She sat up, suddenly chilled, and looked at him. "Where?"

"London first, possibly New York again, then Tokyo. I've stayed too long away from work."

"I see . . ."

He made a harsh sound deep in his throat. "Do you? Richard says you sent for him. Didn't you believe I'd keep the terms of our wager?"

"Of course I believed you would," she said. "I just . . ." She broke off. He was right in a way. She had deliberately forced the issue, so convinced was she that silence between the brothers would only lead to more pain. Now she had to wonder if she had done the right thing.

"It doesn't matter," James said. Despite the sleep he'd had, he still sounded overwhelmingly tired, as though the weight of everything he had been through was only now fully settling over him.

She bit her lip, knowing she shouldn't ask and yet driven to all the same. "Did he say . . . that is, did you ask . . . ?"

He smiled harshly. "Was he behind the kidnapping? No, he wasn't, or so he claims. Strangely enough, I believe him. The terrorists may have settled on me by themselves or it's still possible someone suggested me, but Richard wasn't involved."

"Then why aren't you...? I thought... You should be glad."

"I should be, shouldn't I? But you see, there's one small problem. Richard's desire to clear the air between us was prompted at least in part by a guilty conscience. He did want to unburden himself and for once in my life, I didn't want to listen. I really preferred not to know."

Kristina closed her eyes for a moment, feeling the full burden of her own part in this. She had persuaded James against his better judgment to give his brother a hearing. All the while she'd been praying that Richard truly was innocent, and so he did seem to be, but only up to a point.

"Guilty about what?" she asked faintly. "Not Tessa...?"

He made a harsh sound deep in his throat. "No, of course not. Richard would never feel guilty about something that inconsequential. No, he had another truth to reveal."

He stepped closer to the bed, his eyes bleak. "Apparently, the terrorists did have a particular motive for taking me. They needed cash. Alone among all the hostages who were seized, I was the only one who had wealth. Within days of the kidnapping, Richard was approached. They asked for a very large sum but one that was within the reach of the firm. They seemed to have done their homework at least in that regard."

He paused for a moment and looked away from her. Quietly, he said, "My brother refused. He said that if our positions were reversed, he was certain I would never agree. The irony of it is that he's right. I would have taken the same hard line that he did."

"I don't believe that…" Kristina began. She felt ill. Richard had deliberately left his brother in that hell-hole for four long years, and now here was James saying that he would have done the same. The ruthlessness of it stunned her.

"That's the way I am," he said quietly. "The way I've always had to be. Richard's reasoning made sense. The company could afford the amount the kidnappers wanted, but Richard wasn't certain that would remain the case. He weighed his own ability to keep the business going versus what would be needed to sustain the loss. He decided he couldn't guarantee that the business would survive, and he believed that was what I would want most."

"That's crazy! This was your life. Who cares about the stupid business?"

He shrugged, as though the answer ought to be obvious. "The business employs thousands of people around the world, and it keeps both Wyndham and Innishffarin intact. It's always been my responsibility to assure that that continues. Richard simply acted in my place."

"You aren't like that," she protested. "I've seen an entirely different side of you, much more human, more compassionate." More vulnerable, too, she could have added, but she stopped herself. He would not want to hear that.

"I'm not sure I want to be those things," he said quietly. "I've lived my life a certain way, by certain rules. They can be harsh and there's a great deal they don't allow for but in the end they've always worked."

"They left you trapped in hell for four years! How can you say they work?"

He spread his hands, beseeching her understanding. "They're all I know."

"No," she insisted, "they aren't. If you'd only let yourself admit it, you'd realize that you learned a great deal in those four years. You changed."

"If I do that, they win. The people who did this to me."

"This isn't about winning! For God's sake, it's about your life. You can't go through what you did and not come out the other side a different person. Everything that's happened since you got back proves it."

She sat up higher in the bed, the covers clenched in her hands. Somehow, she had to make him believe her.

"You walked away from Tessa, the woman you were going to marry, without a second thought. That's not the action of a possessive and ruthless man. You left your brother alone even when you were seriously considering the possibility that he'd arranged your kidnapping. And you neglected your business—you admitted that yourself—to be with me. Would the old James Wyndham have done any of those things?"

"Probably not," he admitted slowly.

"Stop lying to yourself. You're hurt because of what Richard did. He was your brother and he didn't protect you. He left you in pain and worse yet, he did it because he was so damn busy trying to be you. To live up to the standard you set. Now he's torn up over it and so are you."

He took a deep breath and stepped away from the bed. "You may be right, Kristina, I just don't know. I can't absorb all of this so quickly. I need time."

She swallowed hard, fighting the pain and the fear. From the depths of her love for him—for she could no longer deny that was what it was—she said, "Then take it. Do what you have to."

The dark slashes of his brows drew together. "No recriminations?"

Slowly, she shook her head. "You've got your rules, I've got mine. Besides, I really believe you'll decide I'm right. The money, the power, everything you and Richard both tried to protect aren't as important as loving and trusting each other. Maybe that sounds naive, but in the end, *that's* what works best."

He seemed to hesitate, as though he truly did want to believe her but his uncertainty was still too great. A moment later, the iron-bound door swung shut behind him.

Chapter 19

She was not going to sit around and brood, on that she was absolutely determined. James was gone and she felt as though he had taken a vital part of herself with him. But life went on.

Work was her refuge. She changed into more sensible clothes—wooden clogs and a plain brown shirt—and set about weeding the vegetable garden. Richard found her there, up to her elbows in spring mud, wacking away at the offending growth and muttering to herself.

"Let me guess," he said as he eyed her indulgently. "You and James have been chatting."

"He's gone," she replied without looking up. There was something very satisfying about pulling weeds out by their roots. It was good, simple work. She didn't have to think about it at all, just do it. Better yet, she didn't have to feel.

"Where to?" Richard asked. He had dropped his languid pose and looked worried.

Kristina shrugged. "London, New York, Tokyo, Timbuktu. Who knows?"

"Did he say why?"

She straightened reluctantly, dusted her hands off and glared at him. "He said he needs time to think. Do you blame him?"

To give Richard credit, he had the grace to look ashamed. Slowly, he shook his head. "I don't blame him for anything. It was my fault."

Despite herself, she felt a sympathetic tug. James wasn't the only one to have suffered for Richard's decision.

"It's odd," she said softly, "I've been telling James all along that we can't deny the past, we have to deal with it. But now I just want it to be over with."

"I'm sorry," he said. "I wish there was something I could do to help."

She managed a weak laugh. "I wish there was, too. But unless you feel like giving me a hand pulling up these weeds, I think we're out of luck."

He gave the weeds a wary look and sighed. "If you really want me to..."

"I was just kidding," she assured him hastily. He actually looked as though he'd do it if she insisted. The thought of him in his very proper pinstripe business suit—the same kind James wore, she realized—getting his nicely manicured hands dirty wrung a smile from her.

"Better get out of here," she advised, "before I remember that the stables need mucking."

"I'm going," he said hastily. As he stepped beyond the vegetable patch, he added, "if you hear from James, will you let me know?"

"If you want me to."

"I do." He hesitated before saying softly, "I'm worried about him."

"You should be used to that by now," Kristina said bluntly. Sympathy only went so far.

He flushed and nodded.

She went back to the weeds. When she straightened up again a few minutes later to rub the back of her neck, he was gone.

By midmorning, she was finished with the gardening. Back in the bailey, she checked on her students and was satisfied that they had fallen into a pleasant routine. The interruption of the banquet had been welcome, but she could see that they were glad to get back to business as usual.

Which left her with a few spare hours. She intended to take full advantage of them. This time she went prepared. Authenticity was all very well but the small flashlight she slipped into her pocket was a whole lot more effective than any pitch torch had ever been. With it and a sharp-edged pick, she intended to explore the small room off the back corridor that had been used as the first keep's chapel.

It was just as she had seen it a few days before, small, dark and unpromising. There seemed very little point in going on. If she hadn't hated giving up so much, she might have done just that.

A quick survey of the room was enough to convince her that the stories about it having been a chapel might well be correct. She could make out the trac-

ings on the stone floor of where an altar could have
stood.

Aside from that, the chamber was completely un-
remarkable. She could find no hint that there was
anything unusual about it... Except...what was that?
There on the floor where it looked as though...

Quickly, she bent over, tracing with her fingers the
large stone set into the floor. Her eyes hadn't fooled
her. Alone of all the stones she had examined, it
showed signs of having been remortared some time
long after the castle was built. Possibly even within the
last few centuries.

But time had taken its toll and the mortar which
would have been strong enough when it was applied
was now beginning to crumble.

Quickly, she got up and left the chapel. When she
returned a short time later, she was carrying the pick.
She put the flashlight down on the floor where its light
would strike the stone. Guided by it, she began slowly
and carefully to crush the mortar.

It was harder work than she'd expected. More than
an hour passed before she was done and even then she
had no idea if she'd accomplished anything or not.
There was only one way to find out.

Dropping the pick, she knelt down again and ran
her fingers around the edge of the stone. With the
mortar gone, she was able to reach down several inches
below the surface of the floor. Her hand found a chink
in the stone. Hardly breathing, she pulled.

She expected nothing. She got far more. Slowly, the
stone rose, pulled by counterweights that must have
been hidden below the floor and which she had just
tripped. As it gave way, she rose quickly and took

several steps back. Where the stone had been was a black hole.

Gingerly, she shone the flashlight into it. She half-expected to learn that she had discovered a dreaded *oubliette*, the hideous pits hapless captives were thrown into, only to be forgotten. But the pit was empty.

A sudden gust of air cooled her skin. She took a deep breath and smiled suddenly. The air smelled of the sea.

She had found the passage to the sea cave where the Wyndham cross had been found.

Excitement gripped her, so intense that it out-weighed prudence. She had a quick image of Katlin Sinclair, the woman who had gone where she was now drawn to follow. With that thought, she gripped the flashlight and bent over the hole, her eyes straining to see where it might lead.

In the back of her mind, she knew that she had to be careful. It would be madness to enter the passage alone. But she had to know... Just a little farther... Yes, there, she thought she could see that the hole did indeed give way to a small passage leading to the east, exactly as it should. If only she could be sure. She inched forward, trying to see through the gloom. Only a little more... a little...

Her balance gave way. She gave a small, muffled scream and fell into darkness.

"She was in the garden this morning," Frank Standish said. "I saw her coming back from there. We thought she was going to have a talk on food preservation techniques, but she didn't show up for it."

James heard him out in silence. He had gotten as far as the airport, had actually gotten onto the plane. With his seatbelt fastened and his notebook computer open in front of him, he'd intended to work through the flight to London.

Instead, he found himself staring out the window as he remembered the last time he'd flown in that direction, with Kristina in the seat beside him, playing gin rummy for all she was worth and beating him shamelessly.

A smile tugged at the corners of his mouth. She could be outrageous, provoking him in all sorts of ways, some of them admittedly very pleasant. She made him reexamine all the presumptions that had guided his life.

No wonder he had run from her.

He stiffened. What was that? He hadn't run. He'd simply needed some time to come to terms with issues that any man would have found difficult. Running had nothing to do with it.

Did it?

Besides, she would be there when he got back.

Wouldn't she?

The sudden thought that she might actually not be there went through him like a lightning bolt. It wasn't possible. She was committed to Innishffarin, to the project.

But she was also a very beautiful and gentle young woman who had feelings of her own.

For the first time, he realized that he didn't know what those feelings were. Certainly, there was passion between them but what else?

Enough to keep her there waiting for him?

Or enough to drive her to leave?

His pilot was an experienced man, chosen in part for his ability to take anything and everything in stride. When his employer informed him that they would have to turn the plane around and head back to the terminal, he did not so much as raise an eyebrow. He merely informed the tower and followed through accordingly.

Which was how James came to be standing in the bailey in late afternoon, glaring at Frank Standish and wondering where the hell Kristina could have gone to.

"Any chance she went into the village?" he asked.

Frank shrugged. "There's always a chance but she did have that talk scheduled. It's not like her to forget. Fact is, I was starting to think we might take a look around when you showed up."

"She couldn't have gone back to the cliff?"

The younger man flushed. "Not likely. I think she learned her lesson. No anomaly is worth getting hurt for."

"No, it isn't. Don't think I've forgotten your part in that. It was the height of poor judgment to . . ." He broke off and frowned. "What anomaly?"

Frank shrugged. He really didn't want the matter of the cliff climb raised again, but it seemed that he didn't have any choice. "She thought she saw something up there. Didn't say much about it but I gather she wanted to take a closer look. Something to do with your family burying something in the cliff." He shrugged again. "I don't know much about it."

He took a quick step back, the better to dodge the sudden stream of rage that poured from James, accompanied by a choice curse or two. All Frank could really make out was something about the "damn treasure."

His ears perked up. "What treasure?"

"The Wyndham Treasure, of course. Didn't she ever say anything to you about it?"

Slowly, Frank shook his head. "Not that I can remember. We talked about the cross but that's all. I mean, that was the treasure, wasn't it?"

"Most sane people think so," James muttered.

Frank hardly heard him. His mind was working overtime. "But, gee, what if it wasn't? I mean, what if there was something more? It would be an incredible coup for Professor McGinnis if she found it." He thought some more and said, "I wonder if this has anything to do with that old book she's always looking at?"

"What book?" James demanded. He could not believe that she would be so foolish, especially not after the cliff. But he had to admit that it was possible.

He had seen her as a woman of gentleness and beauty, but she also possessed great passion, as he had every reason to know. And she wasn't shy about getting her own way, evident in how she had assured that he and Richard would talk.

She had said nothing to him to indicate that she had any great interest in the treasure, but that might have been deliberate. Standish was right. To discover what could conceivably be a horde of medieval artifacts would set the seal on a career she cared a great deal about.

"Show me this book," he commanded.

It was clear that there were few things Standish wanted to do less, but he was not so foolish as to say so. Glumly, he led James toward the small chamber Kristina used. There, in a plain wooden chest, they found Linus's manuscript.

James raised his head slowly. It was several hours later. Day was fading. Outside, he could hear the students going about their chores. A cow lowed softly followed by the plaintive *bah* of a lamb.

His vision was slightly blurred from the effort needed to decipher the elaborate script of the manuscript. All that Latin, he thought wryly, studied through all those years of school. He'd never really expected to have a use for it. Even so, the Latin of the manuscript was far from classical and difficult to understand.

Still, it was an extraordinary experience to read the details of events that had taken place so long ago and yet seemed as fresh as yesterday. Of course, there was a particular reason for that. There had been a party at Innishffarin the day before and two brothers who had reason to be at odds had come face-to-face in what could have been a dangerous confrontation.

But he and Richard had made a kind of peace with each other, as yet incomplete but at least the seeds were sown. For those earlier Wyndhams, the outcome had been far different.

This much, at least, had been accomplished— brother no longer killed brother. There could be pain and anger, but not bloodshed.

So much for progress. Other, less pleasant, truths remained.

She had the book when she came to Innishffarin. Frank had been clear about that when James questioned him again. She'd had the book for some time, going back even before she proposed the Innishffarin project.

And in all that time, she had said nothing about it. Certainly, she hadn't mentioned it to him and if she had told Richard, he would surely have talked about it.

Instead she had kept it to herself. But she had questioned him about the treasure and gleaned the information about the sea cave. And she had actively searched for a way into it when she climbed the cliff face.

"What if she found the treasure?" he asked Frank when he finally found him in a corner of the great hall where he clearly hoped not to be noticed. "What would she do with it?"

"Do?" He thought for a moment and said, "Technically, there's only one thing she could do. Turn it over to you."

"Technically?"

"Well, yeah. I mean Innishffarin is your property so anything found here would also belong to you. The professor knows that. It's true there's a tremendous black market for medieval artifacts, but she wouldn't have anything to do with that."

"You're sure?"

Frank's eyes widened. "Jeez, you're kidding, aren't you? I mean, money's not exactly her thing, in case you haven't noticed. She left a pretty comfortable situation to come here and live like this for months. Besides, she's smart. If all she cared about was bucks, there's plenty of other things she could be doing."

James didn't dispute him but inwardly he was thinking that any sacrifice might seem worthwhile to have a chance at finding a treasure no one else even knew existed.

Having found it—and with no one the wiser—she could do anything she chose.

Anything at all.

Chapter 20

She wasn't going to panic, Kristina decided. Tempting though it was, it wouldn't do her any good. Not that there weren't some very good reasons for giving in to the terror that threatened to overwhelm her at any moment.

She couldn't climb back up the hole. She had tried repeatedly until her hands were torn and bloody, her legs and arms scraped, and her strength gone. No matter what she did, she simply couldn't reach the top. She was trapped at the bottom of it.

Over the centuries, the surface of the passage had sunk, just as the stone floor in the passage had done. Several hundred years before, it might not have been so obvious but now it definitely was. Without a rope or a ladder, there was no way out.

Which made her present position all the more ironic. She had found the place where, she was sure now, Katlin Sinclair had stood when she discovered the Wyndham Cross.

Rainwater and perhaps also the hand of man had long ago carved a small chamber into the side of the cliff. It was just large enough to hold several people. A tall man could have stood upright but his head would brush the ceiling.

Several narrow windows were cut into the side of the outer wall, the one that looked toward the sea. One of these was the window she had seen, the anomaly. The others were hidden by the growth of brushes that had long since covered them over.

She could still make out the pale discoloration on the wall where the cross had hung. It was long since gone. A worn wooden bench remained but it looked so frail that she didn't dare to sit on it.

Apart from that, the chamber was empty.

She had found the hiding place of the Wyndham treasure, just as she'd hoped. Only to also find that there was no treasure left.

As much as she hated to even think of it, she had to admit that she could lose her life in a search for something that had never existed.

A harsh laugh broke from her. It was either that or give in to the urge to cry. What a stupid way to die. What an incredibly foolish waste of life. And just when she had so much to live for. Her impulsiveness, that emotional side of her nature she had always tried to control, might literally be the death of her.

She took a deep breath and wrapped her arms around herself to try to stop her trembling. She wasn't going to think about that. At least not while there was still daylight.

Later, when the dark came, it might be impossible to control her thoughts. But for the moment, she was going to try to make the best use possible of the only chance left to her.

She had to let someone know where she was. Already, she had shouted herself hoarse trying to get attention in the chapel. Now she would try the beach.

There was a chance one or more of her students might decide to go for a walk. With an effort, she managed to pull herself up into the narrow window.

By craning her neck, she could actually see the beach below. But it was deserted and with the rain that had begun to fall, it looked as though it would remain that way.

She slumped back down. Tears burned her eyes. Realistically, she probably couldn't have been heard over the roar of the surf. But letting go of that hope was still very hard.

It brought her face-to-face with the fact that her options were narrowing at an alarming rate. She would have to make her way back down the passage to the chapel and try again to make herself heard.

But when she did, the results were the same. No one came anywhere close enough to the chapel to hear her hoarse shouts. Shudders racked her. The fresh sea breeze that had been so enticing a few hours before had turned cold. Her thin brown tunic offered scant protection.

Slowly, she sank to the ground, her knees drawn up to her chin and her arms wrapped around herself. She would wait a little while and then try again.

There was nothing else she could do.

* * *

"I need a flashlight," James said. He was stripping off his suit jacket as he spoke. Around him the students exchanged worried looks. He had called them together to explain that Kristina was missing.

They would separate into pairs and explore the entire castle and surrounding area. If she wasn't found quickly, searchers would be called in from the manor and the village. It would be dark in less than an hour. They had to work fast.

"And a rope," he added. He wasn't really sure about what he would need but he knew the castle well and understood the dangers. "All of you take the same. Now get going."

They obeyed quickly.

When he was alone, James checked the flashlight to make sure it worked and tested the rope. As he did, he thought rapidly, trying to remember everything he had ever heard about the discovery of the Wyndham Cross.

Katlin Sinclair had been a very young woman when she found it. The castle had come to her through her grandfather, Isaiah Sinclair, but the Wyndhams had always considered it their own. It had been lost to them several generations before as payment for supposed treachery against the throne. They had never given up the hope of recovering it.

Even so, when Katlin came to Innishffarin, Angus Wyndham had welcomed her. In all honesty, he did it because he presumed she couldn't fulfill the terms of old Isaiah's will, namely that she live for six months in what was then a run-down, drafty and thoroughly unappealing ruin. If she failed, Innishffarin became Angus's—and the Wyndham's—once again.

Katlin had surprised him. She'd persevered with courage and fortitude. In the process, she'd won Angus's love as well as his admiration.

How exactly she had come to know the legends about the treasure, James couldn't remember. But she had and finally she had stumbled across the location.

He seemed to recall that she'd been searching for it deliberately. She'd become trapped somewhere. Angus had found her, saving her life and very shortly thereafter, making her his wife.

Trapped. The word made James's blood run cold. For a moment, he could feel the walls of his cell closing around him, shutting out all light, all hope. He couldn't bear to think of Kristina in the same situation. Never mind the anger he felt when he discovered what had really brought her to Innishffarin. He still had to get her out.

But out of where? Where in the vast castle could the treasure have been hidden?

In the cliff above the sea. In a chamber that would have had to exist in the castle's earliest days, back when the cross was hidden. That meant the oldest part of the keep, the part his Viking ancestors had built when they came in their long-prowed ships, liked what they'd found and decided to stay.

The original part of the castle overlooked the sea. There were still remnants there of the first structure. Even a chamber that had been a chapel.

He put the rope over his shoulder, took the flashlight, and headed for the back corridor.

The light struck Kristina full in the face. She blinked and raised a hand to shield her face.

"What . . . ?"

"Kristina, can you hear me?"

James! She couldn't believe it. Her mind must be playing tricks on her. He had gone, leaving her...

"Kristina! Answer me. Are you down there?"

She jumped up, reaching for the light. "Yes!" The sound was little more than a croak. Desperately, she cleared her throat and tried again.

"Yes! James, down here!"

She heard a quick exhalation of breath as though with relief. A moment later, the end of a rope dropped in front of her.

"Grab hold," he called.

She did as he said and moments later was lifted up. When her feet touched the floor of the chapel, her legs gave way. She would have fallen if his arm hadn't been taut around her.

For a long moment, she clung to him, luxuriating in the solid, hard reality of him. He was there, he had found her. She was safe.

"I thought..." Her voice broke. She took a shaky breath and started again.

"I thought you had gone."

"I came back," he said. Gently, but unmistakably, he moved her away from him. His eyes were unreadable as they raked over her. "You were very foolish."

She laughed faintly. "You don't have to tell me. I was so excited when I found the passage, I leaned over too far and fell in."

He started to say that she was fortunate she hadn't been hurt but a closer look made him realize that wasn't the case. There was blood on her hands, her face was bruised, and her arms and legs had deep scratches.

The sight hurt him more than he wanted to admit. It was as though the pain were his own.

"Go and get cleaned up," he said, not looking at her.

She swallowed hard, realizing for the first time that he was furiously angry. She didn't know why but she also didn't feel up to arguing with him. She was overwhelmed by uncertainty.

"All right," she murmured and turned to go. Only to discover that her legs had not regained their strength as she thought they had. She stumbled and fell painfully against the wall.

"Ooohh."

"Damn it!" He lifted her easily and carried her from the chapel. In the small room she used, he left her briefly while he got a bucket of water from the well in the bailey yard. With a soft cloth, he wiped her face, her arms and legs, and the blood from her hands. Before he was done, his own hands were shaking.

"Was it worth it?" he asked gruffly as he dropped the cloth back into the bucket.

"I don't know what...?" Her voice shook. She had managed to lie still under his ministrations but her heart was beating wildly. She still didn't understand why he was there, or why she felt such contrary emotions pouring from him. She sat up.

"You came here to search for the treasure, didn't you?"

At her look of surprise, not to say shock, he grimaced. "Don't bother lying. I know about the manuscript. That's how I found you. If Standish hadn't told me what you were looking for, you'd still be down in that hole."

"You knew I was interested in the treasure. We talked about it."

"Yes, we did, under circumstances that were guaranteed to make me trust you, weren't they? I'd never be more likely to tell you anything I knew than I was then. But I also didn't know you actually intended to search. Richard didn't know either, did he?"

Slowly, she shook her head. She could hardly believe what he was saying. Did he truly believe that she cared so much about the treasure she was willing to seduce him to try to get to it? "I mentioned the treasure to Richard," she murmured, "but he was no more interested in it than you were."

"Convenient for you."

Her mouth tightened. "I don't see it that way. I'm a historian and a teacher. It's only natural that I'd be curious about whether there was anything still hidden here. If there had been, it would have been a tremendous find."

"If...?"

"I found the chamber cut into the cliff where the cross was. There's nothing left there."

"Nothing?"

She shook her head. "It's empty. You were right all along. Linus was wrong. The treasure was the cross."

"You must be very disappointed," he said.

"Right now, I'm too busy being glad I'm alive."

And being glad that he was here with her, although that had faded fast. Anger welled up in her. Damn him!

"You just can't let yourself feel, can you?" she demanded. "You're so damn determined to be *James Wyndham*, no emotions, no weaknesses, no changes. You don't want to admit that your brother let you down, maybe through no fault of his own since he was only following your example. But it hurt all the more because of that, didn't it? And this does, too."

She glared at him, ignoring the tears that were pouring down her cheeks. "You don't want to be vulnerable at all, to have to trust anyone. It's so much easier to just think that everyone's out for himself—or herself. That nothing matters except the damn money and the power, just because you lived that way. Well, damn it, I don't. I have other priorities and I'm only sorry that they scare you so damn much!"

Her vocabulary left something to be desired but she couldn't help that. She had come to the end of her rope.

He could think anything he pleased and do anything he wanted. If he honestly believed that her sole interest had been the treasure, there was no point even trying to convince him otherwise.

"Go away," she said. "Just go away. I don't want to see you."

She kept her head erect and her shoulders squared until she heard him leave. Only then did she give in to wrenching grief.

Chapter 21

"I know you'll manage just fine," Kristina said. "Everything's in good shape. I'll be in New York for three or four days and then I'll stop in Boston briefly. Frank's got the numbers where I can be reached."

She paused for a moment, looking at them all fondly. Her throat was tight. "I hope you understand," she went on, "the chance to raise more funding for the living history project came up very suddenly. I can't ignore it. People willing to support research like this are few and far between. We have to encourage them all we can."

The students nodded in agreement. Most of them were getting through school with a combination of scholarships and loans. She didn't have to convince them how tight money could be.

The interest of a foundation in helping to fund the project could be a godsend, but in more ways than they knew. As much as Kristina hated the thought, part of her reason for returning to the States was to find a replacement for herself at Innishffarin. It was time for her to move on to other things.

It was two days since her discovery of the cliff chamber. She had not seen James since she sent him away but she knew that he was still at Wyndham. At any moment, he might return. She could not bear the thought of facing him again.

Very simply, she was giving up. The crushing experience he had been through and the terrible conflicts it unleashed within him were more than she could heal. And more than she could endure.

She was leaving.

"I'm very proud of all of you," she said softly. "Please remember that."

A few of the students exchanged curious glances but before anyone could comment, Frank stepped in. "We'd better be going, Professor. You don't want to miss the plane."

She gave him a grateful glance and picked up her bag. The Jeep was parked just beyond the drawbridge. She got in and stared straight ahead.

Frank slipped behind the wheel. He gave her a quick, worried look as she turned the ignition.

"You okay?"

"I'm fine. Let's go."

He looked unconvinced but he didn't argue. Moments later, they were on the shore road, heading away from the castle.

Kristina did not look back. Because of that, she did not see the man on the dappled gray stallion who paused briefly on a hillock above the proud stone walls before urging his mount down toward them.

The bailey yard was deserted as James entered. He left the gray horse munching oats in the stable and went into the great hall. A few of the students were there. They nodded cordially as he passed through. There was no sign of Kristina. For the moment, that suited him.

Entering the back corridor, he made his way quickly to the old chapel. The stone block was back in the floor, where he had put it for safety's sake. He raised it, secured the rope he had brought around a stone pillar and threw the other end into the hole. With the flashlight on his belt already lit, he followed.

The cliff chamber was as Kristina had described, bare except for an old bench and there on the wall, the tracings of where the cross had been. Nothing else. Yet, she had been so sure, enough to take a chance that could have cost her her life.

It was easy to believe that she was simply wrong. But in the past two days, unable to think of anything but Kristina, he had found himself consumed by curiosity. Enough so that he was driven to make his own search through some of the oldest volumes in the family library, books no one had looked at for generations.

And it was there, in the sleepless hours of the night, that he found enough to convince him Linus might not have misled her.

Yet there was nothing in the cliff chamber.

He shook his head with frustration. He had wanted this badly as a gesture of apology, forgiveness, reconciliation. As a fresh start between them. In the past, such a notion would have amused him. But now he took it seriously. He had hurt her and he wanted to make amends.

He was reluctant to give up but there seemed no choice. Whatever Linus had thought he saw when the prodigal Wyndham son returned, it had long since vanished into the mists of time.

Or had it? He had been staring down at the rough limestone floor. It was uneven, carved as it had been by the slow trickle of water over eons. But there were also signs that it had been deliberately smoothed at some time, perhaps in a period of troubles to prepare the chamber to be used as a hiding place.

The job had been done well except for that small area over by the window where the floor rose slightly.

He bent closer, staring at it. After a moment, he knelt and ran his hands over the surface. No, he was not mistaken. Long ago, someone had cut out a piece of the soft limestone and then replaced it.

Excitement filled him. His heart was beating rapidly as he carefully eased the stone up. The faint light from the single window illuminated a hole several feet in width. He reached for the flashlight on his belt and flipped it on.

In the darkness, gold gleamed. He shone the light around, hardly breathing. The sight that met his eyes astounded him. He saw what most people would think of as treasure—a magnificent belt of golden links, a chalice set with jewels and the like.

But, too, he saw the gold bindings of leather-bound manuscripts, treasure troves themselves filled with knowledge from a vanished time. All that a long-dead son of Innishffarin had hidden away, only to seal the secret of his own death.

The cross had been left to guard the chamber but all the rest had been so well concealed that not even the intrepid Katlin and Angus had managed to unearth it.

It had taken a woman of the modern world who believed in the lessons of the past to point the way.

He had to find her.

Kristina said goodbye to Frank at the airport. She'd been lucky to get a seat on a flight leaving for New York in less than an hour. He offered to stay with her. She thanked him but said no. She needed the safe anonymity of crowds who would take no notice of the woman alone with her painful thoughts.

After he had gone, she wandered through the terminal, settling finally at a coffee shop. She ordered a cup but sat without touching it. The bustle of people coming and going around her seemed blurred. She felt insulated from her surroundings, as though there were an invisible wall around her.

A wall around and hollowness inside, which left her little more than a brittle shell liable to break at any moment.

She bit her lower lip hard and forced herself to take a sip of the coffee. It was scalding. She'd forgotten that she took it with milk. Grimacing, she set the cup back down.

"Something else, miss?" the girl behind the counter asked.

Kristina shook her head. She paid, picked her bag up and moved on.

Several flights were called but hers wasn't among them. She found a seat in the waiting area but couldn't stay put. Instead, she got up and began to walk aimlessly along the concourse.

The minutes ticked by. Finally, just when she thought she couldn't bear to wait any longer, the loudspeaker blared the news that her flight was boarding.

She walked back to the gate and stood, watching the passengers beginning to board. Her ticket and boarding pass were in her hand. She had only to join the steady stream passing through the door to the plane.

And still she waited, not knowing what kept her rooted in place. The cabin attendant at the gate eyed her curiously.

Any minute, Kristina thought, she'd be pegged as some kind of weirdo and security would be called. That was all she needed.

She was being ridiculous. Her mind was made up, she had to go, the plane was right there. A few quick steps and she would be on it. Tears blurred her vision. She took a deep, shaky breath and picked up her bag.

James rammed the Range Rover into the first parking spot he could find, jumped out and ran. He reached the concourse in time to hear the last call for the New York flight.

Cursing, he ran faster, only just avoiding a baggage handler with a heavily laden trolley, a harried woman with two small children, and a minister. Apologizing to each, he kept going. He reached the departure gate just in time to see the big jet pulling away.

His shoulders sagged. He stood, catching his breath, and trying to figure out what to do next. He could get a seat on the next commercial flight or he could use his own plane. But the small private jet was slower than the commercial ones.

Either way, he would get to New York several hours after Kristina. And by then she would be . . . where?

It didn't matter. Wherever she was, he would find her. He had to.

Abruptly, he decided to use the private plane. It could be fueled and ready in under an hour. The nearest phone he could use to call his pilot was next to a coffee bar in the middle of the concourse. He had almost reached it, was reaching into his pocket for a coin, when he spotted the woman standing a little distance away.

She had her back to him and was looking out the big plate glass window, watching as the New York bound jet taxied to take off. Her pale hair fell around her shoulders. She wore jeans, a cotton blouse, and a simple jacket. There was a carryon bag in her hand.

Slowly, he put the coin back in his pocket. His throat was tight as he walked across the short distance separating them.

"I thought you didn't like to fly."

Kristina heard the voice through the confusion of her thoughts. It took a moment to register. When it did, she gasped and turned so suddenly that the bag she held flew out from her hand, catching James in the shins.

"*Ouch.*" He grimaced and took a quick step back.

"I'm sorry, I didn't realize...you startled me." Her heart was racing. She was caught on a keen edge between dread and delight.

He was rubbing his leg ruefully and keeping a cautious eye on the bag. "Are you hurt?" she asked instinctively.

"Not as much as I deserve to be," he said. He reached out a hand for the bag. "Here, give me that."

She gripped the handle for a moment before realizing the foolishness of that. The plane was gone. She had missed it deliberately. There was no point pretending otherwise.

A glint of gold danced in front of her eyes. She froze, staring at it. "What's that?"

James took her hand, cupping it in his, and dropped the gold links into it. "A belt of some kind, I think. I'm not really sure. That's your department."

She gazed at him for a long moment, taking in the rumpled ebony hair shot through with silver, the web of lines around his startling blue eyes, the firm set of his mouth. He looked as he always did, yet different. More tentative, somehow, even uncertain.

The weight of the gold was heavy in her hand. "Where did you find this?" she asked.

"In the cliff chamber, along with a good deal more. You were right." Quietly, he added, "About a lot of things."

Slowly, with an uncertainty that touched her, he put his hands on her shoulders and drew her just a little closer. "I'm sorry," he said quietly. "Come back."

The first faint glimmers of happiness so great as to be almost frightening stirred within her. But still, she was cautious.

"For this?" she asked, glancing at the golden belt. Once the thought of what it was part of would have thrilled her. Now she felt, not indifferent exactly, but far removed. Other things mattered far more.

"No," James said. "For us."

Chapter 22

"This is incredible," Kristina said delightedly. She was sitting cross-legged on the bed, dressed only in one of James's older shirts, her hair tumbling around her shoulders and what appeared to be a permanent smile on her lips.

On the bed, opened before her, was one of the manuscripts he had found in the cliff chamber.

"It's a medical book," she explained, "probably a translation from an Arabic text. There's a description here of the treatment for stomach disorders that's fascinating. The scholars are going to have a field day with this stuff." Come morning, she would call New York and explain why she had missed the flight. She was sure she would be forgiven, especially when they heard what had been discovered.

"That's great," James murmured wryly. He was thinking—fondly for a change—about the past. There came a time when it was appropriate for a man to look back over his salad days, appreciate them for what they had been, and pack them neatly away.

The women he'd known had all possessed certain characteristics in common. He doubted any of them would have reacted to an old manuscript as though it had come in a velvet-lined box from one of the better jewelry stores.

He stretched out more comfortably in the big bed and continued to watch her. They were in the master suite at Wyndham Manor. It was a rigorously masculine room dominated by a heavily carved four-poster bed with hunting scenes on the walls and a large fireplace. The scent of wood smoke touched the air.

Outside it was night. He could hear the distant calls of owls and the occasional rustle of small animals moving about in the garden. He closed his eyes for a moment, listening to the familiar but so often ignored sounds of home. When he opened them again, Kristina was looking at him.

"Don't let me keep you awake," she said with a grin.

"That's what I like about the woman," he told the air. "A great sense of humor."

"I thought it was my mind you admired."

"Oh, it is," he assured her with a friendly leer. His hand reached out toward her ankle. She laughed and darted off the bed.

James smiled. He watched the provocative wiggle of her bottom as she walked across the room and placed the manuscript carefully on the table that held the other pieces of the Wyndham Treasure they had brought from the castle a short time before. Her hand brushed the gold chalice gently.

"I'm glad you found it," she said softly. "It's more fitting somehow."

James supposed he was glad, too. Finding the treasure was indisputably good, whoever did it.

He thought back to what he knew about the years immediately after the cross was found. There had been a tremendous outpouring of interest and he supposed there would be again. They would have to look seriously at displaying the treasure at Innishffarin and making it available to scholars.

But that could all wait.

"Come here," he said.

She glanced over her shoulder and smiled. But her teasing air faltered as she studied the powerful, masculine body stretched out as nature had intended it, on top of the rumpled covers.

"Has anyone ever told you," she said huskily, "that you're bossy?"

"Never," he claimed with a straight face.

"Maybe no one had the nerve."

"Except you?"

"Oh, yes," she agreed. "Except me." Slowly, she came toward him, flushing slightly for the old shirt hid little from his eyes.

She sat down on the edge of the bed just beyond the reach of his hand and looked at him with playful seriousness. "Maybe you ought to get some sleep."

He looked down the length of his body and raised an eyebrow. "Do I look as though I should?"

The color in her cheeks deepened. "Well, no, but..."

So quickly that she didn't see it, he reached out, his fingers closing around the thin fabric of the shirt, and drew her to him. When she was half sprawled across him, he smiled. "That's better."

"Is it?" she asked faintly. Breathing was getting difficult but she ought to be used to that by now. He had such an overwhelming effect on her, this proud, strong, vulnerable man.

In his arms, she discovered what it meant to be truly alive. That, above all, was the greatest treasure by far.

"Much," he said and ran his hands under the shirt, down the long line of her back to cup her derriere. She gasped softly.

"Much better," he repeated and turned over, drawing her with him.

One by one, he undid the buttons of the shirt and spread it open. His eyes darkened as he gazed down at her full breasts, the nipples puckered and rosy.

Slowly, he lowered his head, but he did not touch her there. Instead, he rained feather light kisses between her breasts, down across her stomach and on the velvety skin stretched taut between her hips.

She trembled beneath his touch. Frantically, her hands stroked his broad, muscular back as she twisted under him.

Their earlier lovemaking had only heightened her need for him. Vividly aware of his strength, she cried out softly.

His mouth was hot and demanding as he took her own, his tongue stroking her inner warmth, filling her with the taste of him, making her yearn for far more.

She could feel the tremors racking his powerful body as he raised his head, looking at her with eyes heavy with passion.

"Don't leave me again," he said. It wasn't a question and she didn't take it as such. He was a man to lead, to command, to bear the responsibility and take the risks other men couldn't handle.

But he was also tempered in the fire of experience. He had learned to accept his own frailties and even to gain strength from them.

"I won't," she said and knew it for the promise it was. Even as her body thrilled to the passion he aroused and the pleasure he gave, she knew they would find a way to bring past and present together in a future that was theirs to be discovered.

She raised her arms, wrapping them around him, and drew him to her.

Epilogue

"Welcome to Innishffarin," Kristina said. She smiled as she surveyed the motley collection of students gathered in front of her. They had all arrived on morning flights, some from the United States, others from various parts of Europe. They looked tired, disheveled, and eager to get started. Also a little apprehensive.

"I know you've all heard a great deal about the living history project," she went on, "but I promise it's not as bad as you think."

There was laughter all around. When it died down, she continued. "You will work hard during your months here and I'm sure there will be many modern conveniences that you'll miss. But you'll also have an invaluable opportunity to learn what life was really like in a different age. I can say with confidence that you'll find it more interesting than any textbooks you might use. Are there any questions?''

There were the usual inquires about the schedule and routine. When she got through fielding them, she directed the students to their quarters and told them to take the rest of the day to get acclimated. Work would start the following morning.

She left them to it and headed for the Range Rover—a new one—that she'd left in the parking lot. A man was standing beside it. Richard smiled as he saw her coming.

"Giving the usual pep talk?" he asked.

Kristina nodded. She linked her arm in his and gave it a squeeze. "They always look scared at first but that changes pretty fast. How are you doing?"

He made a face. "Jet-lagged as usual. I need to talk with James. We're set to make the next round of acquisitions and I wanted to bring him up-to-date in person."

"I'm sure he'll appreciate it," Kristina said even as she thought that it wasn't really necessary. James had stunned everyone—not the least Richard himself—when he announced that he was turning the American side of the business over to his brother, thereby giving himself more time for other pursuits.

In the statement released to the media, he stressed his trust in his brother and his confidence that under his guidance, Wyndham Industries in America would do better than ever.

Barely had the news hit than tongues were wagging even more fiercely over the announcement that Miss Tessa d'Auberville Westerloo and Mr. Richard Wyndham were to be married. The bride and groom would honeymoon briefly before going to live in the States.

"Tessa would have come," Richard said, "but she's only got a couple more weeks to go and she isn't all that comfortable."

Kristina nodded. She and her sister-in-law would never have very much in common but they had managed to build a cordial relationship. When Tessa and Richard's first child was born shortly, Kristina and James would be the godparents.

"I last saw James down on the beach," she said.

Together, she and Richard walked around behind the castle and climbed down the narrow path that led to the shore. Richard paused partway down and looked curiously toward the small windows that had been cleared of undergrowth.

"So that's where it was all the time."

"Hard to imagine, isn't it?" Kristina asked. "All those centuries and no one even guessed. It makes you wonder what else might be hidden."

He laughed and cast her a teasing look. "It makes *you* wonder. Just don't go trying to find anything on your own again. My brother's got enough gray hair."

"He tells me he's earned every one of them," Kristina said with a grin. They reached the bottom of the path and looked down the beach toward the distant shapes of horse and rider.

"It looks as though they've been to the Viking chapel," she said. "It's one of Derrick's favorite spots."

"Growing another historian?" Richard asked.

Still looking at the man now approaching rapidly on the powerful horse, and the small boy held carefully in the saddle before him, she said, "Another Wynd-ham."

Her smile faded as the horse drew up next to them and she got a better look at the small, grubby figure of her son.

"What have you been rolling in?" she asked re-signedly.

"Grass, I think," James said. He lifted the boy from the saddle and held him at arm's length for a moment as he surveyed him. "Leaves, too, some mud, a bit of moss. Just the usual."

Derrick chortled, kicked his coltish legs in the air, and reached for his mother. She took him with mock reluctance and hugged him close.

"Home for you, young man, and a hot bath."

Richard rumpled Derrick's flaxen hair. The boy's clear blue eyes brightened. His uncle was a particular favorite, not in the least because he could always be counted on to play with him.

About to suggest they do exactly that, Derrick hes-itated. "Wait," he said and dug in the pocket of his trousers. Proudly, he pulled out what looked like a stick of wood and offered it to his mother. "See," he demanded.

Kristina took it and glanced at it quickly, only to look back again. "It's part of an antler," she said.

"He found it near the pond," James said proudly, as though his son had performed a rare and marvel-ous trick.

"Did he?" Kristina asked thoughtfully. She turned the bit of antler over in the palm of her hand. With one finger, she brushed away the dirt that partly cov-

ered it and peered more closely. There were faint, incised markings on the bone.

"Will you show me right where you found it?" she
asked Derrick.

Delighted by the interest, he nodded solemnly.

James laughed. "Can I expect you to be as grubby
as our son before long?"

"Probably," she said unperturbed. Their eyes met
in perfect understanding.

Richard looked from one to the other. He sup-
pressed a sigh. His talk with his brother could wait.

"Come along," he said as he held out his hand to
Derrick. "Let's have some tea."

"After his bath," Kristina called but her heart
wasn't in it.

James bent and held out his hand. He lifted her
easily onto the saddle in front of him.

The bright day beckoned, filled with the promise of
love and of all the treasures still to be found in the ancient castle hard by the sea.

*   *   *   *   *